BASEBALL JOE CAPTAIN

OF THE TEAM

BY

LESTER CHADWICK

BASEBALL JOE CAPTAIN OF THE TEAM

CHAPTER I

QUEER TACTICS

"No use talking, Joe, we seem to be on the toboggan," remarked Jim Barclay, one of the first string pitchers of the Giant team, to his closest chum, Joe Matson; as they came out of the clubhouse at the Chicago baseball park and strolled over toward their dugout in the shadow of the grandstand.

"You're right, old boy," agreed Joe—"Baseball Joe," as he was known by the fans all over the country. "We seem to be headed straight for the cellar championship, and at the present rate it won't be long before we land there. I can't tell what's got into the boys. Perhaps I'm as much to blame as any of the rest of them. I've lost the last two games I pitched."

"Huh!" snorted Jim. "Look at the way you lost them! You never pitched better in your life. You had everything—speed, curves, control, and that old fadeaway of yours was working like a charm. But the boys played behind you like a lot of sand-lotters. They simply threw the game away—handed it to the Cubs on a silver platter. What they did in the field was a sin and a shame. And when it came to batting, they were even worse. The home run and triple you pasted out yourself were the only clouts worth mentioning."

"The boys do seem to have lost their batting eyes," agreed Joe. "And when it comes to fielding, they're all thumbs. What do you think the trouble is?"

"Search me," replied Jim. "We've got the same team we had when we started the season. Look at the way we started off: Three out of four from the Brooklyns, the same from the Bostons, and a clean sweep from the Phillies. It looked as though we were going to go through the League like a prairie fire. But the instant we struck the West we went down with a sickening thud. Pittsburgh wiped up the earth with us. The Reds walked all over us. The Cubs in the last two games have given us the razz. We're beginning to look like something the cat dragged in."

"I can't make it out," observed Joe, thoughtfully. "Of course, every team gets in a slump sometimes. But this has lasted longer than usual, and it's time we snapped out of it. McRae will be a raving lunatic if we don't."

"He's pretty near that now," replied Jim. "And I don't wonder. He'd set his heart on winning the flag this season, and it begins to look as though his cake was dough."

"Even Robbie's lost his smile," said Joe. "And things must be pretty bad when he gets into the doleful dumps."

"I thought that when we got those rascals, Hupft and McCarney, off the team, everything would be plain sailing," remarked Jim. "They seemed to be the only disorganizing element."

"Yes," agreed Joe. "And especially when we got such crackerjacks in their places as Jackwell and Bowen. But speaking of them, have you noticed anything peculiar about them?"

"Great Scott!" exclaimed Jim, in some alarm. "You don't mean to intimate that they're crooks, too?"

"Not at all," replied Joe. "From all I can see, they are as white as any men on the team. And they certainly know baseball from A to Z. They can run rings around Hupft and McCarney. But, just the same, I've noticed something odd about them from the start."

"What, for instance?" asked Jim, with quickened interest.

"They seem nervous and scared at times," answered Joe. "Jackwell, at third, keeps looking towards that part of the grandstand. The other day I was going to throw to him, to catch Elston napping; but I saw that Jackwell wasn't looking at me, and so I held the ball. And I've noticed that when he's coming into the bench between innings he lets his eyes range all over the stands."

"Looking to see if his girl was there, perhaps," laughed Jim.

"Nothing so pleasant as that," asserted Joe. "It was as though he were looking for some one he didn't want to see. And the same thing is true of Bowen. Of course he's out at center, and I can't observe him as well as I can Jackwell. But when he's been sitting in the dugout waiting for his turn at bat, he's always squinting at the fans in the stands and the bleachers. The other boys aren't that way."

"This is all news to me," remarked Jim. "I've noticed that they've been rather clannish and stuck close together, but that's natural enough, seeing that they were pals in the minor-league team from which McRae bought them and that they don't feel quite at home yet in big-league company."

"Well, you keep your eye on them and see if you don't notice what I've been telling you about," counseled Joe. "Of course, it may not mean a thing, but all the same it's struck me as queer."

By this time the two pitchers had reached the Giants' dugout, where most of their teammates had already gathered.

It was a beautiful day in early summer. The Eastern teams' invasion of the West was in full swing, and baseball enthusiasm was running high all over the circuit. The Giants, after a disastrous series of games in Pittsburgh and Cincinnati, had struck

Chicago. Or, perhaps, it would be more correct to say that Chicago had struck them, for the Cubs had taken the first two games with ease.

No doubt that accounted for the tremendous throng that had been pouring into the gates that afternoon, until now the stands and bleachers were crowded with enthusiastic fans. For if there was anything in the world that Chicago dearly loved, it was to see the Giants beaten. One game from the haughty Giants, the champions of the world, was more keenly relished than two games from any other club.

The rivalry between the teams of the two great cities was intense, dating from the days when the old Chicagos, with "Pop" Anson and Frank Chance at their head, had been accustomed to sweeping everything before them. Now the tables had been turned, and for the last few years, the Giants, with McRae as their astute manager and Baseball Joe as their pitching "ace," had had the upper hand. Twice in succession the Giants had won the championship of the National League and had wound up the season in a blaze of glory by also winning the World Series.

This year they were desperately anxious to repeat. And, as Jim had said, it looked at the beginning of the season as though they were going to do it. They got off on the right foot and had an easy time of it in the games with the other Eastern clubs.

But with the Western clubs it was another story. A "jinx" seemed to be pursuing them. Pittsburgh had tied the can to them, and the Reds, not to be outdone, had tightened the knot. The Cubs thus far had clawed them savagely. They had tasted blood, and their appetite had grown with what it had fed upon. And for that reason the sport lovers of the Windy City had turned out in force to see the Cubs once more make the Giants "their meat."

McRae, the manager, was sitting on the bench with Robson, his assistant, as Joe and Jim approached. There was an anxious furrow on his brow, and even the rotund and rubicund "Robbie," usually jolly and smiling, seemed in the depths of gloom.

McRae's face lightened a little when he saw Joe.

"I'm going to put you in to pitch to-day, Matson," he said. "How's the old soup-bone feeling?"

"Fine and dandy," returned Joe, with a smile.

"I want you to stand those fellows on their heads," said the manager. "They've been making monkeys of us long enough."

"I'll do my best, Mac," promised Joe, as he picked up a ball preparatory to going out for warming-up practice.

"Your best is good enough," replied McRae.

Joe and Jim went out with their respective catchers and limbered up their pitching arms.

"How are they coming, Mylert?" Joe called out to the veteran catcher, who was acting as his backstop.

"Great," pronounced Mylert. "You've got speed to burn and your curves are all to the merry. That hop of yours is working fine. You'll have them breaking their backs to get at the ball."

McRae, in the meantime, had beckoned to Iredell, the captain of the team.

"Look here, Iredell," he asked abruptly, "what's the matter with this team? Why are they playing like a lot of old women?"

"I'm sure I don't know," replied Iredell, flushing and twirling his cap nervously.

"Don't know?" snapped McRae. "Who should know if you don't? You're the captain, aren't you?"

"Sure," admitted Iredell. "But for all that, I can't always get onto what's in the minds of the fellows. I've talked to them and razzed them and done everything except to lam them. They're just in a slump, and they don't seem able to get out. Some of them think a jinx is on their backs. I'm playing my own position well enough, ain't I?"

"Yes, you are," McRae was forced to admit, for Iredell was one of the crack shortstops of the League, and so far had been batting and fielding well. "But that isn't enough. To be a good shortstop is one thing, and to be a good captain is another. I figured you'd be both. Tell me this. Are there any cliques in the team? Any fellows out to do another or show him up? Any fights in the clubhouse that I haven't been told about?"

"No," replied Iredell, "nothing that's worth noticing. Of course, the boys are as sore as boils over the way they keep on losing, and their tempers are on a hair trigger. Once in a while something is said that makes one of them take a crack at another. But that's usually over in a minute and they shake hands and make up. There aren't any real grudges among the boys that I know of."

"Well, things have got to change, and it's largely up to you to change them," growled McRae. "If the job's too big for you, perhaps somebody else will have to take it. I've often found that a shake up in the batting order will work wonders. Perhaps the same thing's true of a shake up in captains."

The flush in Iredell's face grew deeper and his eyes glinted with anger. But he said nothing, and as McRae turned to say something to Robbie, indicating that the interview was ended, he moved away sullenly from the dugout.

Just then the bell rang as a signal for the Giants to run out for practice. The white uniforms of the Chicagos faded away from the diamond, while the gray-suited Giants scattered to their several positions in the field and on the bases.

Jackwell, who had been standing near Joe while the latter was putting the balls over to Mylert, started to run out with the rest, but suddenly he halted and stood in his tracks like a stone image.

Joe, who, out of the corner of his eye, had noted the action, turned to him in surprise.

"What's the matter, Jackwell?" he asked, eying the new third baseman keenly.

"I—I can't go on," stammered Jackwell.

Joe noted that he had suddenly turned white.

CHAPTER II

A BITTER STRUGGLE

Jackwell's legs were sagging, and Joe, alarmed at his condition and afraid that he was going to fall, put his arm about the baseman's shoulder to support him.

"Brace up, old man," he counseled. "What's come over you?"

"I—I don't know," answered Jackwell, trying desperately to get a grip on himself. "I suddenly felt faint. Everything got black before my eyes."

"Touch of the sun, maybe," said Joe, kindly. "Come over and get a drink of water and then sit down on the bench for a few minutes. I'll ask one of the other fellows to take your place at third for practice."

Jackwell sank down on the bench, while Joe returned to his practice with Mylert, somewhat upset by the incident.

A moment later, Bowen, the new centerfielder, came along, and Jackwell beckoned to him. He sat down beside him, and the two conversed in whispers, casting surreptitious glances at a part of the grandstand almost directly behind the third-base position.

Joe kept his eye on the two men and saw Bowen start violently at something Jackwell whispered to him. His face seemed suddenly to have been drained of every drop of blood, and he shook like a man with the ague.

Just then McRae, who had been having an exchange of repartee with Evans, the manager of the Chicago team, who had chaffed him unmercifully about the playing of the Giants, came back to the dugout. He glanced in surprise at the two players.

"What are you fellows doing here?" he asked sharply, glowering at them. "Didn't you hear the bell ring for practice? Why aren't you in your places on the field?"

"I'm sick, Mr. McRae," replied Jackwell. "I wish you'd put somebody else in my place. I ain't in condition to play to-day."

"I'm in the same fix," put in Bowen. "I feel like thirty cents."

"That's what the whole team's worth," growled McRae. "And even at that price the fellow that bought them would get stung. What do you mean, sick? Are you sick or just lazy, soldiering on the job? You seemed husky enough this morning."

"It—it may have been something we ate at noon," suggested Jackwell, rather lamely. "A touch of ptomaine poisoning, or something like that."

"Of course, I'll play if you tell me to," put in Bowen. "But I don't feel up to my work."

McRae stood for a moment in exasperated study of the two. For some reason their excuses did not ring true. Yet their pale faces and evidently unstrung condition seemed to bear out their words.

"Guess there is a jinx after this team all right," he growled. "You fellows go over to the club doctor and let him find out what's the matter with you. I'll put other men in your places for the present."

They hurriedly availed themselves of the permission, and McRae, after a consultation with Robbie, put Renton in Jackwell's place and sent McGuire out in center to hold down Bowen's position.

Again the bell rang, and the Cubs took their final practice. That they were in fine condition for the fray was evident from the way they shot the ball across the diamond. Dazzling plays and almost impossible catches brought round after round of applause from the spectators. It was plain that the whole team was in fine fettle, and that the Giants had their work cut out for them if they were to win.

The Giants, as the visiting team, were first at bat. Axander, the star twirler of the Cubs, picked up the ball and went into the box with a jaunty air that bespoke plenty of confidence.

"Play ball!" cried the umpire.

Axander dug his toes into the box and wound up for the first pitch.

And while the crowd watched breathlessly to see the ball leave his hand, it may be well for the benefit of those who have not read the preceding volumes of this series to tell who Baseball Joe was and trace his career up to the time this story opens.

Joe Matson had been born and brought up in the little town of Riverside in a middle western state. From early boyhood he had been a great lover of the national game, especially of the pitching end of it, to which he had taken naturally. His coolness, quick thinking, good judgment and powerful arm specially fitted him for the box. He soon became known for his skill as a twirler on his home team, and his reputation spread to surrounding towns. His early exploits and the difficulties he had to encounter and overcome are told in the first volume of this series, entitled: "Baseball Joe of the Silver Stars; or, The Rivals of Riverside."

Later, on his school nine, he overcame the obstacles thrown in his way by the bully of the school and pitched his team to victory over his rivals. His field was widened when he went to Yale, and in an emergency he assumed the pitcher's burden and downed Princeton in a glorious battle.

That victory proved a turning point in Joe's life, for the game had been witnessed by a scout for a minor-league team, always on the alert for talent, and he made Joe an offer to join the Pittston team of the Central League. Joe accepted the offer, and soon climbed to the position of the leading twirler in the League.

Still, he was only a "busher," and his delight can be imagined when, at the end of the season, he was drafted into the St. Louis team of the National League. Now he was really in fast company, and had to test his skill against the greatest twirlers in the country. But the fans were quick to learn that he could hold his own with the best of them.

McRae, the manager of the Giants, one of the ablest men in baseball when it came to judging the ability of a player, determined to get Joe for the Giants. He did get him, and had never ceased congratulating himself on the stroke that brought Joe to his team. He soon became its mainstay, and had been the main factor in winning the championship of the National League and the World Series twice in succession. He was a wizard in the box, and his record as pitcher had never been equaled in the history of the game.

And not only in the box, but at the bat he had proved himself without a peer. He was a natural batsman, timing and meeting the ball perfectly and leaning all the weight of his mighty shoulders against it so that it soared far beyond the reach of the fielders. When he hit the ball it was very often ticketed for a homer, and at every city on the League circuit thousands were attracted to the games not only to see a marvelous exhibition of pitching but to see Matson "knock out another home run." What celebrity he gained by his work in both departments is told in a previous volume, and the way in which he saved the game from scandal when it was threatened by a gang of crooked gamblers is narrated in the last volume of the series entitled: "Baseball Joe Saving the League; or, Breaking Up a Great Conspiracy."

But Joe had won other triumphs than those of baseball. He had fallen in love with Mabel Varley, a charming girl whose life he had saved in a runaway accident, and he had married her at the end of the previous season on the diamond. They were ideally happy.

Jim Barclay, a Princeton man who had joined the Giants, had speedily developed into a pitcher only second to Joe himself. He and Joe had become the closest of chums, and on a visit to Riverside Jim had fallen a victim to the charms of Joe's pretty sister, Clara, and was now engaged to her and hoped for an early marriage.

And now to return to the tense situation on the Chicago ball field, where the Cubs and Giants faced each other in one of the critical games of the series.

Curry, the rightfielder of the Giants, was first at bat. He was a good hitter and was as fast as a flash in getting to first.

Axander shot over a high fast one at which Curry refused to bite, and it went as a ball. Then came a pretty first strike right over the heart of the plate. Axander came back with a slow one that lobbed up to the plate looking as big as a balloon. Curry nearly dislocated his spine reaching for it, and though he connected with it he raised an easy fly, which the Cubs' third baseman caught without moving from his tracks.

Iredell came next to the plate, swinging three bats. He threw away two of them, tapped each of his heels with the other for luck, faced the pitcher and glared at him ferociously.

"Put one over, you false alarm, and see me murder it," he called to Axander.

Axander grinned at him.

"You're the captain of the team, aren't you?" he asked. "Well, you'll be only a lieutenant when I get through with you."

He whizzed one over that Iredell swung at savagely and missed. The next he fouled off, making the second strike. Then came a ball and then a third strike, so swift that Iredell struck at it as it settled in the catcher's glove.

"You're out!" shouted the umpire.

Iredell threw down his bat in chagrin and retired to the bench.

Then Burkett, the burly first baseman of the Giants, strode to the plate. He caught the first ball pitched right near the end of his stick and belted it into the rightfield stands. It looked like a sure homer, and the contingent of loyal Giant rooters burst into a cheer. But the cheer was premature, as the umpire called it a foul, and Burkett, who had already rounded first, returned, disgruntled, to the plate.

"Had your eyes tried for glasses lately?" he asked the umpire.

"That'll be about all from you," returned that functionary. "Another wise crack like that, and it's you for the showers."

Axander's next throw went for a ball. On the next Burkett whaled a sharp single over second. A moment later, however, he was caught napping at first by a quick throw from the pitcher, and the inning ended without a score. Burkett, who found himself in his regular position at first, put on his glove and stayed there, glad enough that he was not near enough to the Giants' dugout to get the tongue lashing that McRae had all ready for him.

"Did you see that boob play, Robbie?" McRae growled. "Did you see the way that perfectly good hit was wasted?"

"Sure, I saw it, John," replied Robson, laying his hand soothingly on the knee of his irate friend. "'Twas enough to make a man tear his hair out by the roots. But the game's young yet and we may have the last laugh. I'm banking heavily on what Joe's going to do to them birds."

Joe in the meantime had walked out to the box. It was a tribute to the admiration that was felt for him by fans everywhere that even the Chicago partisans welcomed his coming with a hearty round of applause. He was more than a Giant standby. He was the idol of all true lovers of the national game.

Burton, the heaviest slugger on the Chicago team, was first at bat. Joe looked him over and then sent the ball over for a perfect strike. It came in like a bullet. Burton did not even offer at it.

"Strike one!" called the umpire.

The next one had a fast hop on it, and Burton swung six inches beneath it.

"Strike two!"

Burton set himself for the next one, and succeeded only in fouling it off. Mylert got the ball and returned it to Joe on the bound. The latter caught it carelessly and then, without his usual wind-up, sent it whistling across the plate. It caught Burton entirely off his guard, and his futile stab at it caused even the Chicago fans to break into laughter.

"Out!" cried the umpire, and the discomfited Burton retired sheepishly to the bench.

"That's showing them up, Joe," called up Larry Barrett from second.

"Why didn't you soak that first ball?" demanded Evans, the Chicago manager. "It was a beauty, right in the groove."

"Aw," growled Burton, "how can I hit a ball that I can't see? That came like a shot from a rifle. I ain't no miracle man."

Gallagher came next and had no better luck. One strike was called on him, and the other two he missed.

"Look at that boy, John," exulted Robbie, his red face beaming. "He's got them fellows buffaloed right from the jump. He's making them eat out of his hand. He's skinning 'em alive."

"Fine work," agreed McRae, his anxious features relaxing somewhat. "'Twas the best day's work I ever did when I got him on the team. He's a whole nine by himself. And—blistering billikens! Look at that!"

The "that" was a hot liner that Weston had sent right over the box. Like a flash Joe had leaped into the air and speared it with his gloved hand. The force of the hit was so great that it knocked him down, but he came up smiling with the ball in his hand.

There was a moment of stupefied silence, and then the stands rocked with applause, contributed by the Cub as well as the Giant rooters. That play alone was worth the price of admission.

Joe drew off his glove and came in from the box, while the Chicagos ran out to take their places in the field.

"Great stuff, Joe," cried Jim jubilantly, as he hit his chum a resounding whack on the shoulder. "They didn't have a chance. Keep it up and you'll have those Cubs crawling into their hole and licking their wounds."

"Oh, it will do for a start," said Joe, modestly. "But that's only one inning out of nine, and those fellows may break loose any time. But if our fellows will only give me a run or two, I'll try to hold them down."

But the wished-for runs did not materialize in the Giants' second turn at bat. Wheeler made a strong bid for a run when he sent the ball on a high line between right and center, but the Chicago rightfielder was off at the crack of the bat and just managed to get his hands on the ball and shut off what seemed to have all the earmarks of a homer. It was a sparkling catch and evoked rounds of applause from the Chicago rooters.

McGuire dribbled a slow one to the box that Axander had no trouble in getting to first on time. Renton was an easy victim on strikes.

"Looks as if you'd have to win your own game, Joe," grumbled McRae. "These boobs have more holes in their bats than a chunk of Swiss cheese."

In the Cubs' half Joe mowed them down as fast as they came to the bat. His curve and hop ball were working to perfection. He varied his fast and slow ones with such cunning that he had his opponents up in the air. It was just a procession of bewildered batters to the plate and then back to the bench. It looked as though Joe were in for one of the best days of his brilliant career.

In the third inning the Giants at last broke the ice. Barrett lay down a well-placed bunt along the third base line that the Cub third baseman got all mixed up on in his efforts to field. When at last he did get his hands on it he threw wild, and Barrett easily reached second before the ball was retrieved.

It looked like the possible beginning of a rally, and instantly all was commotion on the Giants' bench. McRae himself ran out to the coaching line near first, while he sent Jim over to third. The Giant players began a line of chatter designed to rattle the Cub pitcher.

But Axander only smiled as he took up his position in the box. He was too much of a veteran to let his opponents get him fussed. But his smile, though it did not entirely disappear, lost some of its brightness when he saw that Baseball Joe was the next man to face him.

Cries of encouragement rose from Joe's mates and from the Giant rooters in the stands.

"Oh, you home-run slugger!"

"Give the ball a ride!"

"Show him where you live!"

"Send it to kingdom come!"

Amid the babel of cries, Joe took up his position at the plate. His brain was alert and his nerves like steel.

"Sorry, Matson, but I'll have to strike you out," said Axander, with a grin. "All Giants look alike to me to-day. Giant killer is my middle name."

"Don't waste any sympathy on me," retorted Joe. "You can send flowers to my funeral later on. But first give me a chance at the ball."

Axander wound up and put one over the corner of the plate with all the force he could muster. Joe caught it near the end of his bat and sent itsoaring out toward rightfield. It was a mighty clout, but when it came down it was just about six inches on the wrong side of the foul line.

Joe, who was well on his way to second, came back and again took up his position at the bat.

But that tremendous hit had given Axander food for thought. The next ball that came over was so wide of the plate that the catcher had to jump for it.

Another ball followed in the same place, and the stands began to murmur.

"He's afraid to let him hit it!"

"He's going to walk him!"

"Matson's got his goat!"

But Axander had resolved to play safe, and the next ball was so wide that it was plain he was doing it with deliberate design.

"Thought you were a giant killer," jeered Joe. "Have you lost your nerve? I can see from here you're trembling."

Stung by the taunt, Axander put all the stuff he had on the ball and sent in a swift incurve.

Joe timed it perfectly. There was a terrific crash as the bat met the ball, and the next instant Joe had dropped the bat and was running to first like a deer.

CHAPTER III

THROWN AWAY

On went the ball almost on a dead line to center, but rising as it went as though it were endowed with wings. On and still on, as though it would never stop. The centerfielder had cast one look at it, and then he turned and ran toward the distant bleachers in the back of the field. He took another look over his shoulder and then threw up his hands in a gesture of despair.

The ball cleared the bleacher rail, still going strong, and finally came to rest in the top row, where it was hastily gobbled up and concealed by an enthusiastic bleacherite, anxious to retain a memento of one of the longest hits ever made on the Chicago grounds.

Joe rounded first, going like a railroad train, but as he saw where the ball was going he moderated his speed in order to conserve his wind and just jogged around the bases until he reached the plate, where Barrett had preceded him.

Again and again he was forced to doff his cap in response to the shouts of the crowd, who had forgotten all partisanship for the moment in the excitement of that mighty homer. And his teammates mauled and pounded him until he laughingly made them desist, and made his way to the bench, where McRae and Robbie were beaming.

"I've been thirty years in baseball, Joe," said McRae, "and I've seen lots of home runs. But if any one of them was finer than that whale of a hit, I've forgotten it."

"If it hadn't been for the bleachers in the way, the ball would be going yet," grinned Robbie. "That swat will break Axander's heart."

But the heart of the Cub pitcher was made of stouter material than Robbie gave it credit for, and Axander settled down and prevented further scoring for that inning. But the Giants had two runs to the good, and the way Joe was pitching made those two runs look as big as a house.

For the next two and a half innings the game developed into a pitchers' duel. Neither side was able to tally, although a scratch hit put a Giant on first and a passed ball advanced him to second. It seemed quite possible that the game would end with the score still two to none.

Joe came up again in the sixth, amid cries by the Giant rooters to repeat. But Axander was going to take no more chances. The memory of that screaming homer still lingered. The catcher stood wide of the plate, and Axander deliberately pitched four bad balls, regardless of the jeers of the crowd.

It was the finest kind of a compliment to Joe's prowess, but he was not looking for compliments. What he wanted was another crack at the ball. There was no help for it, however, and he dropped his bat and trotted down to first.

He watched Axander like a hawk, took a long lead off the bag, and on the second ball pitched started to steal second. He would have made it without difficulty, but the Cub catcher threw the ball to the right of the bag, and the second baseman, in order to grab it, had to get in the way of Joe. There was a mix-up as they came together, and both went down. The baseman dropped the ball, and Joe managed to get his hand on the base before the ball could be recovered.

But when Joe attempted to get up on his feet, his left leg gave way under him, and he had to steady himself by catching hold of Holstein, the second baseman. The latter looked at him in surprise.

"Trying to kid me?" he asked.

"Not at all," replied Joe. "My leg's gone back on me. Must have wrenched or twisted it, I guess, when we came together."

The umpire saw that something had happened and called time, while McRae, Robbie, and the other men on the Giant team gathered around their injured comrade in alarm and consternation.

"Nothing broken, is there, Joe?" cried McRae, as he came running out to second.

"Nothing so bad as that," answered Joe, summoning up a smile. "Guess it's only a sprain. But I'm afraid it puts me out of the running for to-day. I can scarcely bear my weight on it."

The club trainer, Dougherty, ran his hands over Joe with the dexterity of an expert.

"No breaks," he pronounced. "But a wrench to the leg and the ankle sprained. No more work for you, Joe, for a week, at least. Here, some of you fellows help me get him over to the clubhouse."

"Maybe after a little rest and rubbing I can go on with the pitching," suggested Joe.

"Nothing doing," replied Dougherty, laconically. "Get that right out of your noddle. Your work's done for the day."

A rookie was put on second to run for Joe, and the latter was assisted to the clubhouse, where Dougherty and his assistants set to work on the leg and ankle at once.

Gloom so thick that it could have been cut with a knife came down on the Giants' bench. Here was another proof that the "jinx" was still camping on their trail.

But there was no time for grizzling then, for the game had to go on. Jim and Markwith were sent out to warm up, while the Giants finished their half of the inning.

Joe's hit had not gone for nothing, for Ledwith, the rookie, got to third on a fielder's choice, and came home on a long sacrifice fly to center. Iredell swung viciously at the ball and sent up a towering skyscraper that Axander was waiting for when it came down. The inning was over, and, despite the injury to their star pitcher, another run had been stowed away in the Giants' bat bag.

McRae selected Jim to finish the game in his chum's place.

"Go to it, Barclay, and show them what stuff you're made of," admonished the manager. "The boys have given you a lead of three runs, and all you've got to do is to hold those birds down."

"I'll pitch my head off to do it," promised Jim.

He only permitted three men to face him in the Chicago's sixth inning. All the attempts of the Cub coaches and players to rattle him at the send-off resulted in failure.

Mollocher, the first Cub at bat, let a speeder go past because it was a trifle wide. The next was a slow curve that the umpire called a strike. Mollocher looked surprised, but apart from glaring at the umpire made no protest. He laced out at the next one and fouled it to the top of the grandstand for a second strike. The next ball he hit on the upper side, and it went for a harmless hopper to Barrett, who fielded him out at first.

Greaves, who came next, refused to offer at the first, which was high and went as a ball. The next cut the plate for a strike. He fouled the next two in succession, and finally sent a looping fly to Renton at third.

Lasker stood like a wooden man as Jim sent over a beauty for the first strike. The second came over below his knees, and was a ball. He struck at the next and missed, and then Jim fanned him with a slow outcurve that he almost broke his back in reaching for.

It was good pitching, and showed that the Giants had more than one string to their bow. The score was now 3 to 0 on even innings, and, with only three more innings to go, it looked as though the Giants were due to break their long run of hard luck.

"You're doing fine, Jim," encouraged Robbie. "Just keep that up and we'll not only beat 'em but rub it in by giving 'em a row of goose eggs."

"Knock wood," cautioned McRae, giving three sharp raps with his knuckles on the bench. "For the love of Pete, Robbie, cut out that kind of talk. The game isn't over yet by a long shot."

Axander, as cool as an iceberg, put on extra speed and set down the Giants in their half in one, two, three order. Not a man reached first, and the last two were disposed of by the strike-out route.

"Stretch" was the word that ran through the stands as the Chicagos came in for their half of the "lucky seventh," and the crowd rose as one man and stretched while cries of encouragement went up for their favorites.

The charm failed this time, however, for though they gathered one hit off Jim, it counted for nothing, as the next three went out in succession. Jim was certainly pitching airtight ball.

But in the latter half of the eighth, after the Giants had failed to add to their score, there came one of the sudden changes that illustrated once more the uncertainty of the national game.

The head of the Cubs' batting order was up, and their supporters were frantically urging them to do something.

Burton did his best, and sent up a high fly to Curry at right. It looked as though it were made to order for the latter, who did not have to budge from his tracks. The ball came down directly in his hands—and he dropped it!

A mighty roar went up from the crowd, who had looked upon it as an easy out, which it should have been, and Burton, who had slowed up a little, put on speed, rounded first and started for second.

Curry, rattled by his error, fumbled at the ball, and when he did recover it lined it in the direction of second. But it went wide of Barrett, and though Jim, who was backing him up, caught and returned it, Burton was already on the bag.

Gallagher, the next man up, popped a Texas leaguer that Burkett and Barrett ran out for.

"I've got it," cried Barrett.

"It's mine," shouted the burly first baseman.

Each unfortunately believed the other and held back, waiting for his comrade to make the catch. As a result, the ball dropped between them and rolled some distance away.

Burton, who had held the bag, started for third. Burkett retrieved the ball and without getting set hurled it to third. It went high over Renton's head and rolled to the stands. Burton kept right on and crossed the plate for the first run of the game. Gallagher, in the general excitement, reached second.

Pandemonium broke loose among the Chicago rooters.

"We've got them going!" was the cry.

"All over but the shouting!"

Evans, the Chicago manager, sent in his best pinch hitter, Miller, and put a fast rookie, Houghton, on second to run in the place of Gallagher, who was of the ice-wagon type.

To give his comrades time to recover somewhat from their demoralization, Jim stooped down to lace his shoe. He was a long time doing this, and then was very deliberate in taking his place on the mound.

He whizzed over a high fast one that Miller struck at and missed. The next he fouled off. The third just missed cutting the corner of the plate, and it went for a ball. On the next, Miller lay down a bunt that rolled slowly along the third base line.

It looked as though it were going to roll foul, and Renton gave it a chance to do so. However, it kept on the inside of the line, and by the time Renton had gathered it up, Miller had easily reached first.

Wallace went to the bat with orders to wait Jim out, trusting to the hope that the latter would by this time be rattled, because the breaks of the game seemed to be going against him. But when two beauties in succession cut the corners of the plate for strikes, while he stood there like a wooden Indian, he changed his mind.

To make him hit into a double play, Jim made the next an outcurve. Nine times out of ten the batter hits that kind of ball into the dirt. It ran according to form this time also. Wallace hit a grounder that went straight to Larry Barrett at second. Larry set himself for the ball, while Iredell ran over to cover the bag for a double play.

But just before the ball reached Barrett, it took a high bound, went over his head and rolled out into centerfield. Gallagher scored, Miller reached third, and Wallace got to second on a long slide, just escaping being nipped by McGuire's return of the ball.

With two runs in, no one out, and a man each on second and third, it looked bad for the Giants. A single hit would probably score both of the occupants of the bags. Even two outfield sacrifice flies would do it.

The din was tremendous as the crowds yelled in chorus, trying to rattle the already shaky visiting team. But the noise subsided somewhat as Jim put on steam and set down Mollocher on three successive strikes.

Greaves came up next, and lashed out at the first ball pitched, sending a grasser toward first. Burkett made a good pick-up, stepped on the bag, putting out Greaves, and then hurled to Mylert to catch Miller, who was legging it to the plate. But although Mylert made a mighty leap, the ball went over his head and before it could be recovered both Miller and Wallace had crossed the plate, making the score four to three in favor of the Chicagos.

And the Chicago rooters promptly went mad!

CHAPTER IV

FROM BAD TO WORSE

That nightmare inning came to an end without further scoring, as Jim struck out Lasker on four pitched balls. Then, with a sigh of relief, Jim pulled off his glove and went in to the bench, while a sheepish and disgruntled lot of Giants followed him in for their last inning. McRae was white with anger, and had no hesitation in telling the team what he thought of them.

"You bunch of four-flushers!" he stormed. "Throwing the ball all around the lot like a gang of schoolboys. You fellows are Giants—I don't think. You're a disgrace to your uniforms. You're drawing your salaries on false pretenses. Letting those fellows get four runs in a single inning without making a real hit. What do you want the pitcher to do—strike out every man that comes to the bat, while you go to sleep in the field? You make me tired. You ought to join the Ladies' Bloomer League. And even then Maggie Murphy's team would put it all over you. Go in there now and get those runs back."

With their faces burning from the tongue lashing of their irate manager, the Giants went in for their last inning.

Larry was first up and cracked out a sharp single to right that looked at first as though he might stretch it to a double, but it was so smartly relayed that he found it advisable to scramble back to the initial bag.

Jim was next up. The first two balls pitched were wide of the plate and he refused to bite. The next one, however, he caught right on the seam for a liner that went whistling into right for a double.

Larry had started at the crack of the bat, and had rounded second by the time Jim got to first. He kept on to third, where Iredell was on the coaching line. There he should have been retained, for Burton, who was renowned for his throwing arm, had by this time got the ball and was setting himself for the throw. Iredell, however, urged Larry on, with the consequence that when he slid into the plate the ball was there waiting for him. Jim, in the meantime, had reached second.

Larry picked himself up, brushed himself off and went to the bench, muttering growls against Iredell for having egged him on. Had two men beenout there might have been some excuse for taking the chance. But with none out, it was almost certain that, either by a hit or a sacrifice, he could have been brought in with the run that would have tied the score.

Mylert tried to kill the ball, but hit it on the under side and it went up in a high fly that was easily gobbled up by the Cubs' first baseman.

Curry, the last hope of the Giants, came to the bat. He was in a frenzy of eagerness to redeem himself, as it was his inglorious muff that had started the Cubs on their way to those four unearned runs.

Axander himself was beginning to feel the strain, and was a bit wild. Curry looked them over carefully and let the bad ones go by. A couple of good ones were sandwiched in, at which he swung and missed.

With three balls and two strikes, both pitcher and batter were "in the hole." Axander had to put the next one over under penalty of passing the batter. And if Curry missed the next good one, the game was over.

Axander wound up and let one go straight for the plate. Curry caught it full and fair and the ball soared off toward left.

Weston, the Cub leftfielder, was off with the crack of the ball, running in the direction the latter was taking. It seemed like a hopeless quest, but he kept on, and just as the ball was going over his head he made a tremendous leap and caught it with one hand. He was off balance and turned a complete somersault, but when he came up he still had hold of the ball. It was a catch such as is seldom seen more than two or three times in a season.

The game was over, and the Cubs had triumphed by a score of 4 runs to 3. The crowd swarmed down on the diamond to surround and applaud their favorites, who had plucked victory from the very jaws of defeat, or, to put it more correctly, had accepted the game which the Giants had generously handed over to them.

It was a sore and dejected band of Giants that made their way to the clubhouse. The end had come so suddenly that they could hardly realize what had happened. Some were inclined to blame the "jinx," but the more intelligent knew that their own errors and those of some of their comrades had alone brought about their downfall. The defeat was all the more exasperating, because they had had superb pitching throughout—pitching that would have won nine games out of ten and would certainly have won that one if their twirlers had been given half-way decent support.

"Hard luck, Jim," was Joe's greeting to his comrade, as the latter came in and made ready for the showers. "You pitched a dandy game. It's tough when four runs come in without one of them being earned."

"All in a day's work," replied Jim, affecting a cheerfulness that he was far from feeling. "But you're the one I'm worrying about. How's that leg and foot?"

"Dougherty says it will be all right in a week," replied Joe. "He's rubbed most of the soreness out of them, but I'll have to favor them for a while."

"Glory be!" exclaimed Jim with fervor. "If you were out of the game for a long time it would be all up with the Giants. Then they'd go to pieces for fair."

"Not a bit of it," disclaimed Joe. "It's too great a team to be dependent on any one man. I'm only just one cog in a fine machine."

"Looked like a rather wobbly machine this afternoon," said Jim, ruefully.

"Sure," agreed Joe. "The boys did play like a bunch of hams. But every team does that once in a while. The boys will shake off this slump, and then they'll begin to climb. Remember that time when we won twenty-six straight? What we've done once, we can do again. I'm not a seventh son of a seventh son, but I have a hunch that we're just about due to do that very thing."

"I hope you're as good a prophet as you are a pitcher," replied Jim, grinning. He was beginning to find Joe's optimism contagious.

Their conversation was interrupted by the coming of McRae. A sudden silence fell over the occupants of the clubhouse, for they knew the danger signals, and a glance at the manager's face told them that a storm was brewing.

"Giants!" exclaimed McRae, and they winced at the bitter sarcasm in his tone. "Where have I heard that word before? A fine bunch of pennant winners! Why, you couldn't win the pennant in the Podunk League. Put you up against a gang of bushers, and they'd laugh themselves to death. Any high school nine would make you look foolish. Giants? Dwarfs, pigmies, runts! Easy meat for any team you come across! Champions of the world? Cellar champions! Sub-cellar champions! Just keep on this way, and the other teams will bury you so deep you'll be coming out in China. I'm going to change my name. I'm ashamed to be known as the manager of such a bunch of dubs."

Nobody ventured to interrupt the tirade, partly because they felt that he was justified in his anger and partly because no one cared to play the part of lightning rod. When McRae was in that mood, it was best to let him talk himself out.

From the general roast he came down to particulars. He glared around and singled out Curry. That hapless individual evaded his glance and pretended to be very busy in tying his shoe.

"You're the one that started that bunch of errors in the eighth inning," McRae shouted, pointing an accusing finger at him.

"Aw," muttered Curry, "any one can make a muff once in a while."

"It isn't for the muff I'm calling you down," retorted McRae. "I know that can happen to any man, and I never roast any one for it. Why, we lost the World's championship one year in Boston when Rodgrass made that muff in centerfield. I never said a word to him about it, and in the next year's contract I raised his salary. What I'm panning you for is that rotten throw that followed the muff. That's when you lost your head. You could easily have caught Burton at second and stopped the rally.

"And you, Burkett," he went on, turning to the first baseman. "For a man who calls himself a major leaguer, you certainly went the limit this afternoon. Don't you get sleep enough at night that you have to go to sleep on first? And those wild throws, one over Renton's head and the other over Mylert's. Oh, what's the use," he continued, throwing his hands in the air. "I've got a doctor on this club that can take care of any bone in the leg or bone in the arm, but he can't do anything with bones in the head."

If they thought he had worn himself out, they were greatly mistaken. He turned to Iredell.

"Come outside, Iredell," he said, "I want to have a word with you."

Once outside the clubhouse, he turned a grim face on the captain.

"I didn't want to call you down before your men, Iredell," he snapped, "because I didn't care to weaken the discipline of the team—that is, if there's any discipline left in the club. But I want to tell you that if your work to-day is a sample of the way you captain the team, why, the sooner there's a change in captains the better."

"I don't know just what you mean," muttered Iredell, an angry red suffusing his face.

"You know perfectly well what I mean," declared McRae. "How about that ball that fell to the ground between Larry and Burkett? Either one of them could have got it. Why didn't they?"

Iredell remained silent, fingering his cap.

"Because you didn't call out which was to take it," McRae himself supplied the answer. "Their eyes were on the ball, and when each said he could get it each left it to the other. All you had to do was to call out the name of one of them, and he'd have got it. That's what you're captain for—to use your judgment in a pinch.

"Then there was that rotten coaching at third base," McRae went on with his indictment. "Why didn't you hold Larry there? You know what a terror Burton is on long throws to the plate and that he'd probably get him. With nobody out, it was a cinch that one of the next three batsmen would have brought Larry in. And with him dancing around third, he might have got Axander's goat. Then, too, the infield would have been drawn in for a play at the plate, and that would have given a better chance for a hit to the outfield. Am I right or am I wrong?"

"I suppose you're right," conceded Iredell. "But a fellow can't always think of everything. If Larry had got to the plate, you'd be patting me on the back."

"No, I wouldn't," snapped McRae, "because it would have been just fool's luck. Why, I fined a man twenty-five dollars once for knocking out a home run when I had ordered him to bunt. That he came across with a home run didn't change the fact that at that point in the game a bunt was the proper thing, and nine times out of ten would have gone through. You've got to use your sense and judgment and do the thing that seems most likely to bring home the bacon."

"I don't seem to please you these days, no matter what I do," said Iredell sullenly.

"You'll only please me when you do things right," returned McRae. "You know as well as any one else that I never ride my men. I've been a ball player myself as well as manager, and I can put myself in the place of both. But what I want are men who are quick in the head as well as the feet. Give me the choice between a fast thinker and a fast runner, and I'll take the fast thinker every time. Look at Joe Matson, the way he shot that ball over on Burton to-day before he knew where he was at. He's always doing something of that kind — outguessing the other fellow. His think tank is working every minute. He puts out as many men with his head as he does with his arm. And that's what makes him the greatest pitcher in this country to-day, bar none.

"Now, take it from me, Iredell, that's the kind of thinking that's going to pull this team out of the mud. I'm paying you a good salary to play shortstop. There, you're delivering the goods. But I've tacked a couple of thousands onto your salary to act as captain. There, you're not delivering the goods. And those goods have got to be delivered, or, by ginger, I'll know the reason why!"

CHAPTER V

A STARTLING SUGGESTION

With this ultimatum, the irate manager stalked off to join Robbie, while Iredell, his face like a thunder cloud, returned to the clubhouse.

Nor was his wrath at the "roasting" he had received at the hands of McRae lessened by the consciousness that it was deserved. He knew in his heart that he had neglected his duties, or, at least, had failed to take advantage of his opportunities. The game might have been won if he had been on the job. To be sure, the team had played like a lot of bushers, but that did not relieve him of his responsibility. It was when they were playing badly that it was up to him to step into the breach. And that was what he had lamentably failed to do.

"Look at the face of him," whispered Larry to Wheeler. "The old man has been giving him the rough edge of his tongue."

"And when that tongue gets going it can certainly flay a man alive," remarked Wheeler. "I'm sore yet from what he gave the bunch of us. Let's hurry and get out of this. It's too much like a funeral around here to suit me."

McRae in the meantime was unburdening his heart to Robbie. The latter was his closest friend and adviser. They had been teammates in the early days on the old Orioles of Baltimore, when that famous team had been burning up the League. Both of them knew baseball from beginning to end. Together they had worked out most of the inside stuff, such as the delayed steal, the hit and run, and other clever bits of strategy that had now become the common property of all up-to-date major-league teams.

Yet, though as close friends as brothers, they were as different in temperament as two men could be. Robbie caught his flies with molasses. McRae relied on vinegar to catch his. Robbie knew how to salve the umpires. McRae was on their backs clawing like a wildcat. McRae ruffled up the feathers of his men, while Robbie smoothed them down. Each had his own special qualities and defects. But both were square and just and upright, and commanded the respect of the members of the team. Together they formed an ideal combination, whose worth was attested by the way they had led the Giants to victory. Into that wonderful team they had put the fighting spirit, the indefinable something that made them the "class" of the League and more than once the champions of the world. Even when they failed to win the pennant, they were always close to the top, and it was usually the Giants that the winning team had to beat.

Just now, however, the Giants were undeniably in the slump that at times will come to the best of teams, and both McRae and Robbie, who were hard losers, were at their wits' end to know how to get them out of it.

"We're up against it for fair, Robbie," said McRae, as they walked to the gate on their way to the hotel at which the Giants were stopping. "Think of the way the Chicagos are giving us the merry ha ha! We just gave them that game to-day. Looked as though we had it sewed up for fair. People had started to leave their seats, thinking it was all over. Then we turn around and hand the game over to them."

"It's tough luck, to be sure," Robbie agreed. "If Matson hadn't been hurt, we'd have copped it sure. They couldn't get within a mile of him. And now as the capsheaf, he's probably out of the game for a week. But cheer up, Mac. The season's young yet, and we've got out of many a worse hole than this."

"It wasn't so much the boys going to pieces in that one inning that makes me so sore," returned the manager. "Any team will get a case of therattles once in a while and play like a lot of dubs. What gets my goat are the blunders that Iredell made. As a captain, supposed to use his brains, he did well—I don't think."

"It was rotten judgment," agreed Robbie, thoughtfully. "And what makes it worse is that it isn't the first time it's happened. He's overlooked a lot of things since we started on this trip. Some of them have been trifling and haven't done much damage. Some of them the spectators wouldn't notice at all. But you've seen them and I've seen them."

"And what's worse, some of the team have seen them," returned McRae. "That's taken some of their confidence away from them and made them shaky. A captain is a good deal like a pitcher. If he's good, the team play behind him like thoroughbreds. If he's poor, they play like a lot of selling platers. I shouldn't wonder if that's the whole secret of this present slump."

"Perhaps you're right, John," assented Robbie. "We'll have to coach Iredell, wise him up on the inside stuff, and see if he doesn't do better."

McRae shook his head.

"That won't do the trick," he replied. "A good captain is born, not made. He's got to have the gray matter in his noddle to start with. If he hasn't got it, all the coaching in the world won't put it into him. It's a matter of brains, first, last and all the time. I've come to the conclusion that Iredell hasn't got them. He's got a ball player's brains. But he hasn't got a captain's brains, and that's all there is to it."

"Well, admitting that that's so, we seem to be up against it," mused Robbie, ruefully. "Who else on the team is any better in that respect? Run over the list. Mylert, Burkett, Barrett, Jackwell, Curry, Bowen, Wheeler. I don't know that any one of them has anything on Iredell in the matter of sense and judgment."

"Haven't you overlooked some one?" asked McRae, significantly.

Robbie looked at him in wonderment.

"Nobody except the substitutes," he said. "And of course they're out of the question."

"How about the box?" asked McRae.

"Oh, the pitchers!" returned Robbie. "I didn't take them into consideration. But of course a pitcher can't be captain. That goes without saying."

"Not with me it doesn't go without saying," said McRae. "Why can't a pitcher act as captain?"

"Why — why," stammered Robbie, "just because it isn't done. I don't remember a case where it ever was done."

"That cuts no ice with me at all," declared McRae, incisively. "Whatever success I've had in the world has been got by doing things that aren't done. How was it that we made the old Orioles the class of the League and the wonder of the baseball world? By doing the things that aren't done — that no other team had thought of. They went along in the old groove, playing cut and dried baseball. We went after them like a whirlwind with a raft of new ideas, and before they knew where they were at, we had their shirts."

"Wriggling snakes!" exclaimed Robbie, his face lighting up, as he gave his friend a resounding slap on the back. "Mac, you've got me going. You're the same old Mac, always getting up something new. Matson, of course! Joe Matson, not only the greatest pitcher, but the brainiest man in all baseball! Matson, who thinks like lightning. Matson, that the whole team worships. Matson, who can give any one cards and spades and beat him out. Mac, you old rascal, you take my breath away. You've hit the bull's-eye."

McRae smiled his gratification.

"That's all right, Robbie, but you needn't go knocking me down with that ham of a hand of yours," he grumbled.

"Have you mentioned the matter to Joe yet?" asked Robbie, eagerly.

"Not yet," replied the manager. "I wouldn't do that anyway until I had talked the matter over with you and learned what you thought of it. And then, too, with that bruised leg and ankle of his, he won't be in the game for a week or so, anyway. So you really cotton to the idea, do you?"

"I fall for it like a load of bricks," was the response. "Of course, Matson's yet to be heard from. It's a pretty heavy responsibility to be placed on a man that's already carrying the team along with his wonderful pitching. Perhaps he'll think it's a little too much to ask of him."

"I'll take a chance on that," replied McRae, confidently. "He's got a marvelous physique, and he always keeps himself in the best of condition. He's strong enough to carry any load that he's asked to bear. Then, too, you know how he's wrapt up in the success of the team. He's never balked yet at anything I've asked him to do. He's playing baseball not only for money, but because he loves it. He talks baseball, thinks baseball, eats baseball, dreams baseball. He's hep to every fine point in the game and he's on the job every second. And when it comes to thinking fast and acting quickly — well, you know as well as I do that nobody can touch him."

"He's a wizard, all right," agreed Robbie. "But here's a point to be thought over, John. A captain's got to be in every game. Joe pitches perhaps two games a week."

"I've thought of that, too," McRae replied. "On the days he's not in the box, he can play in the outfield. And think of the batting strength that will add to the team. He's liable to break up any game with one of the same kind of homers he knocked out to-day. He's as much of a wonder with the bat as he is in the box, and that's going some."

"Better and better," declared Robbie, exultantly. "Mac, I take off my hat to you. You've hit on an idea that's going to win the pennant of the League this season, with the World Series thrown in for good measure. Who cares for to-day's game? Who cares if the Giants are in a slump? Just make Joe Matson captain of the team and then see the Giants climb!"

CHAPTER VI

PERPLEXING PROBLEMS

"I hope you're right, Robbie," replied McRae, "and I believe you are. But not a word about this to anybody yet until we've mulled it over in our minds from every angle and are ready to spring it. I don't want Iredell to get any inkling of it yet, for then perhaps he'd get sullen and indifferent and things will be even worse than they are now."

"I'll keep it under my hat," promised Robbie. "How do you think Iredell's going to take it? He's an ugly sort of customer, you know, when he gets roiled."

"I guess he'll be easy enough to handle," returned McRae. "I'll let him down easy and heal his wounds with a little increase in salary. But whether he does or not, I'm not going to let any one's personal ambitions stand in the way of the success of the team. That comes before anything."

"Well now, to change the subject," said Robbie, "who are we going to put in the box to-morrow? We've got to have that game, or the Chicagos will have a clean sweep of the series."

"I guess we'll have to depend on Markwith," replied McRae. "The Chicagos have never been able to do much against his southpaw slants. Other things being equal, I'd put Barclay in the box. But he pitched the last part of to-day's game, and perhaps it will be too soon to ask him to repeat. Even at that I may take a chance. I'll see how they warm up before the game."

"It's too bad that Matson was hurt in to-day's game," remarked Robbie. "We were counting on him to take at least two games from St. Louis. Barclay, perhaps, could take another. Three out of four would help us some in winding up the trip. But if they trim us, too, as all the other Western teams have done, I'll hate to go back and face the New York fans."

"I'll work Jim in two of them," said McRae. "Markwith, Bradley and Merton will have to help him out. Possibly Joe will be in shape for the last game. And maybe the team will take a brace and wake up. At any rate, we can only hope. There isn't much nourishment in hope, but it's all we've got."

In the meantime, Jim and Joe had finished their dressing and were preparing to leave the clubhouse.

Jackwell and Bowen were the only occupants left in the place. They were sitting in a corner engaged in earnest conversation.

"How is the leg, Matson?" asked Bowen, as the two chums passed near them.

"None too good," returned Joe. "But it doesn't feel as sore as I feel inside to see that game go flooey. Pity you fellows weren't in it. McGuire and Renton weren't so bad in the field, but they're not as good stickers as you fellows, and your bats might have turned the tide. By the way, are you feeling any better now?"

"I'm all right," answered Jackwell, a little confusedly.

"I'm not feeling exactly up to snuff," said Bowen. "But I guess I'll be able to go in to-morrow."

"Ptomaine poisoning's a pretty bad thing," said Joe, looking at them rather quizzically. "It usually hangs on for days. You're lucky to get over it so quickly."

"You look fit as a fiddle," added Jim, dryly. "Or is it the hectic flush of disease that gives you such a good color?"

"I guess it was only a slight attack," said Jackwell. "Just enough to put us out of our stride for the day."

"I've got to get to the hotel and get there quickly," declared Joe, a twinge going through his foot as he stepped down from the threshold of the clubhouse. "Mabel will be at the hotel, wondering what on earth has happened to me."

"By jiminy, that's so!" cried Jim, turning to stare at his chum. "What will you think of me, old boy, if I confess that in the excitement of the game I'd forgotten about her coming?"

Joe grinned.

"You wouldn't have been so quick to forget if Clara had been able to come along with her," he said, as he walked along gingerly, favoring his injured leg.

"Say, Joe, that leg must be pretty bad," said Jim, anxiously. "Better rest a while, don't you think, before starting out?"

"I tell you I've waited too long already," returned Joe. "Just call a taxi, will you? and we'll spin down to the hotel in no time."

Jim went personally in search of a conveyance. It was not hard to find one, and he returned almost immediately to find Joe limping toward him with the aid of a cane furnished by Dougherty. The latter had offered him his shoulder, but Joe, with a smile, refused.

"I may be a cripple, but I refuse to be treated as such," he told Jim, in response to the latter's protest. "Next thing you know, they'll be offering to carry me on a stretcher."

Nevertheless, Jim noted that Joe sighted the taxicab with eagerness, and leaned back in its shabby interior with a sigh of relief.

"Hate to show myself to Mabel in this shape," he said ruefully. "Looks as though I'd had the worst end of the fight."

"Rather step up lively to the tune of 'Hail the Conquering Hero Comes,' I suppose?" said Jim, with an understanding grin. "I think I get your train of thought all right, old man. But I wouldn't worry, if I were you. Nothing you could do would ever make Mabel think you anything but a hero."

"Let's hope you have the right dope," said Joe.

He looked abstractedly from the dingy windows of the cab at the spectacle of the crowded streets. At that moment he really saw nothing but his young wife as she had looked the last time they had been forced to say good-bye. It had seemed to him then that he could never bear to part from her again. He was so eager to get to her that he had a ludicrous desire to get out and push the taxicab along.

"Thought it was to-night that Mabel was coming," remarked Jim, interrupting his reverie. "You could have met her at the train then."

"Reggie found that he would have to come to the city on business, and since it was necessary for him to come on an earlier train, Mabel decided to change her own plans so that she could come along with him," explained Joe.

"Oh, so we're about to see our old friend, Reggie, again!" exclaimed Jim, with real enthusiasm. "Glad to see the old boy, though I can't help wishing he'd mislay that monocle of his. 'The bally thing makes me nervous, don't you know?'" he finished, in perfect imitation of the absent Reggie.

Reginald Varley not only had the fact that he was Mabel's brother to recommend him to Joe and Jim, but despite his affectation of a supposed English accent and the absurdity of a monocle, Reggie was a fine and likable fellow.

For his part, Reggie professed a great admiration for the chums, especially for his brother-in-law, Baseball Joe. When he could help it, he never missed an opportunity of following the exploits of the two, and, therefore, he had been grateful on this occasion to business for furnishing him an excuse for accompanying his sister to Chicago while the Giants were still there.

"Suppose we go light on this accident, Jim," suggested Joe, indicating his injured leg and foot. "Just a slight sprain you know."

"I get you," returned Jim, adding, as his suddenly startled gaze leaped to the traffic that whirled past the rapidly moving taxicab: "Look at that car coming toward us. On the wrong side of the street, too! That driver's either drunk or crazy!"

Instantly Joe took in the danger. A big automobile, being driven at terrific speed, had rounded the corner on two wheels and was charging down upon them. It seemed that the driver of their taxicab would be a superman if he should prove able to avoid a terrible accident.

Jim had opened the door as though to jump, but Joe called to him.

"Sit tight, Jim," he gritted. "It's the only way."

Lucky for them that the taxi man was keen witted. He saw the only thing that was possible to do in such an emergency, and did it without hesitation.

With a wild bumping of wheels and screeching of emergency brake, the car skidded up on the sidewalk, slithered along for a few feet and came to a standstill. The oncoming car had missed the rear wheels of the taxicab by the fraction of an inch!

Pedestrians, sensing the imminent peril, had scattered wildly, and now returned vociferously to view the curious spectacle of a taxicab planted squarely in the middle of the sidewalk.

Joe's relief at the narrow escape from disaster changed immediately to impatience with the rapidly gathering and gaping crowd.

"More delay! Say, Jim, can't we beat it out of here?"

"Fine chance! Especially with your game leg," Jim retorted, adding with a chuckle: "Here comes a cop. Watch him get rid of the crowd."

"More likely to arrest us for disorderly conduct and disturbing the peace," said Joe, disconsolately. "Fine husband Mabel will think she has. She'll think I'm mighty anxious to get to her."

"Don't be such a gloom hound," laughed Jim. "This cop has a pleasant face. Wait till I give him some blarney."

At that moment the policeman, having interviewed the sullen and angry chauffeur, opened the door of the cab. The constantly gathering crowd pressed forward curiously to get a glimpse of Joe and Jim.

The officer, a round-faced, good-natured-looking individual, stared at Joe for a moment and then broke into a broad grin.

"Begorry, if you ain't the livin' image of Baseball Joe, the greatest slinger in captivity, my name ain't Denny M'Lean!"

"Sure, it's Baseball Joe! And we owe the fact that he's still living to the quick wits of our friend here," broke in Jim, indicating the still furious chauffeur. "That fool in the other car was driving on the wrong side of the road, officer— —"

"Sure he was!"

"I saw it myself!"

"Looked like a head-on collision, I'll tell the world!"

These and other cries came from the crowd, among whom the news that the great Baseball Joe occupied the cab with another famous twirler had spread like wildfire.

"Do me a favor, will you, officer?" urged Joe, taking out his watch and glancing at it hastily. "I'm already late for an appointment. Clear the road, will you, and let us get going?"

"So far as I see, there ain't no particular objection to that," returned the bluecoat, with exasperating deliberation. "The sidewalk ain't no proper parkin' place for an automobile, as you know. But as you seem to be havin' plenty of witnesses that say ye couldn't have done no different, 'twill be easy to overlook yer imperdence. Now thin," turning to the crowd, "did any one of ye notice the license plate of that law-breakin' car?"

Several persons came forward with more or less reliable information. After making a note of this, while Joe fumed with increasing impatience, the officer returned and grinned at them, his eyes snapping with humor.

"Lucky for McRae of the Giants that Baseball Joe kept a whole skin on him this day. When I get that truck driver I'll be tellin' him what I think of him in no unsartin terms. Good-bye to yez, and good luck."

He thrust his huge paw inside the cab, and Joe gripped it heartily. For many years after this meeting with the great Giant twirler, Sergeant Dennis M'Lean was to exhibit proudly the hand that had been gripped by Baseball Joe.

They were off at last, crawling through the close-packed crowd, and with tremendous relief found themselves once more part of the traffic, speeding toward the Wheatstone Hotel where Mabel and Reggie were waiting for them.

"Suppose we'll have a few blowouts now, just to make the thing real good," grumbled Joe, and Jim laughed.

"Here we are before the Wheatstone now," he said. "Just goes to show how sound your gloomy prophecies are!"

Joe's heart leaped as he saw the great building which he was making his headquarters during the stay of the club in Chicago and where he had also engaged a room for Reggie. He started to leap from the cab, which had slowed at the curb, but a sharp twinge from his injured leg reminded him of his partly crippled condition.

"Take it easy, old man," warned Jim. "If you don't favor that foot, you may find yourself laid up for a month instead of a week."

It was all very well for Jim to say "take it easy," but when a young married man has been separated from his wife for weeks, the thing isn't so easily done.

They rode in the elevator to the fifth floor where, leaning on his cane and refusing the help of Jim's arm, Joe got out and hobbled down the corridor to the door of his apartment.

"Remember, I'm not really hurt, I just imagine I am," he cautioned Jim once more, as he put his hand on the knob.

Instantly the door opened and a vision of bright hair and rosy face seized him by the hand and dragged him into the room.

"You too, Jim! Come in, do!" cried Mabel, breathlessly. "Reggie and I have been waiting ages for you. Joe — Joe, dear — that cane! You — —"

"It's nothing, nothing at all, little girl," soothed Joe, his arms about her. "Just a little spill on the field. Be all right in a week. Ask Doc Dougherty, if you don't believe me."

Mabel held him off anxiously at arm's length and looked appealingly at Jim.

"Is he telling me the truth? Is he?"

"Well, I like that!" said Joe, before Jim could answer. "As if I didn't always tell you the truth?"

"You know, I never make it my business to interfere in the quarrels of husband and wife," drawled the familiar tones of Reggie, as, attracted by the sound of voices, he strolled in from the other room. "In fact, quarrels of any kind are foreign to my gentle disposition, don't you know. But on this occasion, I really feel called upon to interrupt. Jim, my dear fellow, how is the old bean to-day? Rippin', from the looks of it, what? My word, brother-in-law," turning to Joe and adjusting his monocle so as to scrutinize him the better, "you have been indulging in a fisticuff of some sort, yes? Tried to do for the old teammates, did you?"

"Oh, leave him alone, Reggie, do!" protested Mabel, all tender solicitude, as she led Joe to a chair and forced him into it. "Can't you see he is all tired out? Now don't talk, dear, unless you want to," she added to Joe, placing a cushion behind his head and looking at him anxiously, her pretty head on one side.

Joe heaved a contented sigh and smiled up at her.

"As long as you don't tell me not to look at you, I don't care!" he said.

CHAPTER VII

BAD NEWS FOR JIM

"My word, I do believe they have forgotten us completely," said Reggie, plaintively, as he placed his monocle in his eye and stared at the absorbed young couple. "Perhaps we had better be making ourselves scarce, Jim, old chap."

"Nothing doing," retorted Jim, moving a chair up toward Joe and Mabel and placing himself in it as though he intended remaining there indefinitely. "I don't stir a step from this place until Mabel tells me all the news from home."

"He means all the news about Clara," laughed Joe, as Mabel obediently sat down beside him and turned her attention to Jim.

"Oh, Clara is all right," said Mabel, but in spite of her cheerful words, the others saw that a cloud had darkened her face. "It is Mother Matson I am worrying about," she added slowly.

Mrs. Matson, Joe's mother, had lately been in poor health. Because of this fact, Mabel had stayed with her mother-in-law for a time after hermarriage to Joe. But recently she had yielded to the urging of her own family to visit them in Goldsboro, North Carolina, her old home. Although Mabel had been busy renewing old friendships there, she had kept in almost daily touch with Mrs. Matson and Clara through the mails. As a matter of fact, Jim had more than once complained that Mabel heard a great deal more from his fiancée than he did himself. Owing to the constantly changing address of the team, Jim's mail, as well as Joe's, was often delayed.

Because of Mrs. Matson's illness, Clara had postponed her marriage with Jim, hoping for her mother's restoration to health. Until that happy time came, nothing remained to Jim but to possess his soul in patience, which was often very hard to do.

Now, at Mabel's mention of his mother, Joe started forward, fixing his anxious gaze upon his wife.

"What has happened to mother?" he demanded. "Is she—nothing serious, is it?"

"Oh, no, no!" said Mabel, patting his hand soothingly. "There is nothing fatally wrong. She is—oh, I might as well tell you at once, Joe dear, for you would only worry the more if I tried to keep things from you. It is feared that Mother Matson must undergo an operation, a rather serious operation, I am afraid."

"What for?" asked Joe, quietly, although his face had become suddenly white.

"Clara didn't say in her letter," returned Mabel, soberly. "Your family doctor, Doctor Reeves, is calling a consultation. Clara will undoubtedly write more fully after that is over."

"A consultation!" cried Joe, leaping to his feet, only to slump down again in his chair at the pain in his injured leg. "Why, this is horrible, girl! Do you know when they expect to—do it?"

"They certainly won't operate right away, Clara says," Mabel returned. "They think her heart is too weak to stand the ordeal just now. Dr. Reeves is going to put her through a special course of treatment, and he thinks that in a month or two she will be ready."

"My poor mother!" groaned Joe. "How can I go on playing ball with that thing in prospect? I got a letter from mother a day or two ago," he added, feeling in the pocket of his coat for the note from home. "She didn't say anything about any trouble then."

"Of course she wouldn't, you old silly," said Mabel, gently. "Don't you know that mothers always worry about everybody else but themselves? Mother Matson never would take her illness seriously, you know, and if she had she would have been the very last one to worry you with it. It was Clara, not your mother, who decided you ought to be told now and asked me to do it."

"That sure is tough luck, Joe," said Jim, gravely. "I had no idea your mother was as sick as that."

"But, I say, don't pull such a long face over it, old chap," urged Reggie, trying to strike a cheerful note in the general gloom of the place. "People are operated on, you know, some of them again and again, and come up smilin' in the end. It's a bally shame and all that, but no need giving up hope altogether, you know. Hope on, hope ever, as the poet sings. Now, I knew of a person once who had a complication of diseases—most distressin'—and the doctors insisted that there must be an operation. But when the day came for the operation, old chap, they found——"

"Spare me the details, will you, Reggie?" urged Joe. "I can't go them just now."

"Certainly, old chap, certainly," agreed Reggie, with swift compunction. "I might have known the subject would be, well, distasteful to you. To change the topic of conversation, just cast your eye for a moment in the direction of our old friend, Jim. He is dyin' to learn more about Clara, you know, and can't for the life of him decide how to tell you about it. How about it, old chap? Am I right?" Saying this, he tapped Jim playfully with his monocle, and the latter reluctantly smiled.

"You sure are a mind reader, old boy," he said. "I must confess that a little first-hand news of Clara would be welcome, and Mabel's seen her since I have."

Joe, looking at Mabel at that moment, was again surprised to find her eyes shadowed and anxious. The expression passed in a moment, however, and she smiled upon Jim reassuringly.

"Clara was dreadfully disappointed at not being able to be here with Reggie and me, and of course she is worried to death about Mother Matson, but aside from that she's all right."

"No news of any kind?" urged Jim, regarding Mabel closely. It seemed to Joe that Jim also had noticed the faint hesitation that had crept into Mabel's manner at mention of Clara's name. "Even the smallest scrap of news, first hand, would be mighty welcome, you know."

Mabel seemed to hesitate, then got to her feet and walked over to the window. The boys watched her uneasily, but when she turned back to them her face was bright and untroubled.

"I wish I had some news, Jim," she said, in her normal tone. "But you must remember that I have been in Goldsboro for some time, and the only news I get of Clara is through the mails. But now I think I've been answering questions enough," she added lightly, a hand on Joe's shoulder. "I think I will start asking a few in my turn. First of all, I want to know just how you happened to get hurt, Joe."

Despite the fact that, just then, he wished to talk about nothing so little as about himself, Joe recounted as quickly as he could the details of his accident. From that the conversation turned to the condition of the team and the discouraging slump it had taken.

"We sure seem to be headed straight for the bottom," remarked Jim, adding, as he looked ruefully at Joe: "And now with our champion twirler laid up for an indefinite period, things look pretty tough for the Giants. If only Jackwell and Bowen would quit looking over their shoulders and watch the ball, we might have a chance to rattle the jinx that's after us."

Both Mabel and Reggie—the latter was an ardent baseball fan and fairly "ate up" anything that concerned the game—demanded to know more about Jackwell and Bowen, and there ensued an animated discussion as to the meaning of the peculiar actions of the two men.

It was Reggie who finally repeated his suggestion that he and Jim "toddle on" in order to leave Joe and Mabel a few minutes of private conversation before joining them again for dinner.

Joe did not protest very hard, for he was aching to have Mabel to himself. He was very anxious about his mother, and more than a little curious to know what, if anything, was amiss with Clara.

Mabel came to him herself as soon as the door was closed behind Jim and Reggie. She held out her hands to him and Joe took them gently.

"What is it, little girl?" he asked. "You were holding back something about mother and Clara. Now suppose you tell me."

"Oh, Joe, I am so worried. I've told you everything about poor mother. But Clara — well, I think she ought to be soundly scolded!"

For the first time since he had heard of his mother's illness, Joe's grave face relaxed in a smile.

"Who's going to do it — you?" he chaffed. "You never scolded me but once, and then I liked it."

"But you don't take me seriously, and this really is serious, Joe," said Mabel, her pretty forehead marred by an anxious frown. "If you could see this fellow with his handsome eyes and his beautiful clothes — —"

"What fellow?" interrupted Joe, becoming suddenly interested. "You don't mean — —"

"Yes I do, just that!" returned Mabel, shaking her head solemnly. "This Adonis I'm talking about is pestering Clara with his attentions."

"Give me his name," cried Joe. "I'll soon show this little cupid where he gets off — —"

"He isn't little, Joe. He's broad-shouldered and six feet tall and he has a million dollars — maybe ten million for all I know — —"

"What's his name?" roared Joe again, with undiminished ire. "What do I care if he's twenty feet tall and has a billion dollars? Hang around my sister, will he?"

"Oh, hush, Joe, hush!" cautioned Mabel, putting a finger to his lips and looking apprehensively toward the door. "Some one will be coming in to see where the fire is."

Joe took her hand gently away and looked at her intently.

"What is there behind all this?" he asked quietly. "Clara doesn't encourage this fellow, does she? She wouldn't do that?"

Mabel looked troubled.

"I hope not, Joe. Oh, I hope not!" she said, and for a moment there was silence while the two studied the pattern of the rug upon the floor, busy with troubled thoughts. It was Joe who again broke the silence.

"You haven't told me his name yet," he reminded Mabel, quietly.

"His name is Tom Pepperil. He used to live near Riverside, but he went away for a long time and made a fortune. Now he has come back, and,according to Clara's letters, is making desperate love to her."

"But she has no right to listen to him! She's Jim's!"

Mabel glanced up at him swiftly and then down at the pattern of the rug again.

"No," she said. Then, after a long minute, she came close to Joe and put her hand over his again.

"Wouldn't it be dreadful," she said, "if the worst we fear should happen, and she should give up good old Jim for that fellow, whose chief recommendation is his money?"

"I couldn't bear to think of it," groaned Joe. "I'd rather lose every cent I have in the world than have it happen. Tell me that you don't think it will ever come to that!"

"I don't know, Joe," said Mabel, sadly. "She's so tantalizingly vague. Perhaps it's the strain she's under on account of mother that makes her so different from her usual self. I can't understand Clara any more."

There was a long silence, and then Joe roused himself to ask dully:

"Do you think we ought to tell Jim?"

CHAPTER VIII

THE HIDDEN-BALL TRICK

"Oh, I wouldn't tell Jim!" exclaimed Mabel, in alarm. "In the first place, we're not clear enough about what Clara means to do. Perhaps it won't amount to anything after all. And if it does, it'll be bad enough when it comes without our doing anything to hasten it."

"I can't understand it," said Joe, gloomily. "There never seemed to be two people more perfectly made for each other than Jim and Clara—always excepting ourselves," he hastened to add, as he pressed her hand—"and it will be one of the greatest blows of my life if there should be any break between them. Clara seemed to be dead in love with Jim; and as for him, he fairly worships the ground she walks on. When he gets one of her letters, he's dead to the world. And he's one of the finest fellows that ever breathed. I look on him as a brother. He hasn't any bad habits, is as straight as a string, a splendid specimen of manhood, handsome, well educated—what on earth could any girl ask for more? And he's making a splendid income too. Has Clara suddenly gone crazy?"

"It's beyond me," replied Mabel. "Clara is the dearest girl, but just now I'd like to give her a good shaking. Lots of girls of course are dazzled by millions, but I never believed Clara would be one of them. And perhaps she isn't, Joe dear. We may be doing her a great injustice. We'll have to wait and see."

"Well, promise me, anyway, that you'll write to her at once," urged Joe. "I'd do it myself, but you girls can talk to each other about such things a good deal better than any man can. Try to bring her to her senses and urge her not to wreck her own life and Jim's simply for money or social position. She'd only be gaining the shadow of happiness and losing the substance."

"I'll write to-morrow," promised Mabel. "But now let's dismiss all unpleasant thoughts and remember only that we're together."

While Joe was desperate at the injury to his foot that kept him out of the game just at a time he was sorely needed by his team, he found some compensation in the fact that he could spend more time with Mabel than would otherwise have been possible. He did not have to take part in the morning practice, and in the afternoons he and Mabel attended the games together as spectators.

On the other hand, Mabel was deeply disappointed that she could not see Joe pitch, as she had joyously counted on doing. She was intensely proud of her famous young husband, and was always one of the most enthusiastic rooters when he was scheduled to take his turn in the box. More than once Joe had won some critical game because of the inspiration that came to him from the knowledge that Mabel was looking on. But there was no use murmuring against fate, and they had to take things as they were, promising themselves to make up for their disappointment later in the season.

Reggie, too, felt that fate had treated him unfairly.

"Why, to tell the bally truth, old topper," he declaimed to Joe, "I didn't have to come to Chicago at all, don't you know! I just drummed up the excuse that I ought to look over our branch in this city, and the guv'nor fell for it. It's rippin', simply rippin', the way you've been pitchin' and battin' ever since the season opened, and I'd been countin' on seem' you stand the blighters on their heads. And just when I got here, the old leg had to go bad! It's disgustin'!"

"Hard luck, old boy," laughed Joe. "But you'll see many a game yet through that blessed monocle of yours. If you feel sore, think how much sorer I am and take comfort."

The crowning disgrace of having the Cubs take four games in a row was happily spared the Giants. McRae put in Jim again, and this time the team gave him better support and he pulled out a victory.

"Great stuff, old man," congratulated Joe, as Jim, after the game, came up to the box in which Joe and Mabel were sitting.

"You pitched beautifully, Jim," was Mabel's tribute, as she smiled upon him.

"Awfully nice of you to say so," responded Jim, in a sort of lifeless way. "But most of the credit was due to the team. They played good ball to-day. Guess I'll go and dress now and see you later."

Joe and Mabel looked at each other, as Jim stalked away across the diamond to the clubhouse.

"Doesn't seem very responsive, does he?" remarked Mabel.

"No, he doesn't," said Joe thoughtfully. "Generally he's bubbling over with enthusiasm after the Giants have won. He's been very quiet since our talk last night."

"Do you think he suspected there was anything wrong?" asked Mabel, anxiously.

"I shouldn't wonder," answered Joe somberly. "He's quick as a flash to sense anything, and I noticed a shadow on his face as he watched you when we were talking about Clara. Hang it all!" he burst out, with a vehemence that startled Mabel. "If Clara throws him down, I'll never forgive her, even if she is my sister. What's the matter with the girls nowadays, anyway? Haven't they any sense?"

"Some of them have," answered Mabel. "Myself, for instance. That's the reason I married you, Joe dear."

"For which heaven be thanked," responded Joe, with a fervor that left nothing for Mabel to desire. "I'm the luckiest fellow on earth. And just because I am so happy, I want Jim to be happy too.

"Then, there's another thing," he went on, "which, while it's infinitely less important than Jim's happiness, is important, just the same. That is the effect it will have on the chances of the Giants. We never needed men to be in shape to do their best work as much as we need them now. And the most important men on any team are the pitchers. I'm not saying that because I'm a pitcher, but because it's a simple fact that every one knows. Let the pitchers go wrong, and the best team on earth can't win. And a pitcher that has a load of trouble on his mind can't do his best work. How do you suppose Jim can keep up to his standard if Clara does her best to break his heart?"

"I suppose that's true," assented Mabel. "And yet I thought he pitched well to-day."

"He doesn't know all we know," replied Joe. "He just has a suspicion, and he's trying to assure himself that it's groundless. But even at that, he wasn't in his usual form this afternoon. You may not have noticed it, but I did. He got by because the boys played well behind him and because the Cubs let down and played indifferent ball. But he wasn't the old Jim. Already that thing is beginning to work on him. And if the worst happens, it will break him all up—at least, for the present season. If I had that sister of mine here this afternoon, I'll bet she'd hear something that would make her ears burn."

Mabel soothed him as best she could, but her own heart was heavy as she thought of the possibilities that the future held in store for poor Jim.

From Chicago the Giants went to St. Louis, the last stop on their Western schedule. Here they had some hopes of redeeming themselves and making up for their recent failures, for the Cardinals were going none too well. Mornsby, their famous shortstop, had had a quarrel with the manager, and was seeking to get his release to some other team, any one of which would have snapped him up at a fabulous price. There were rumors of cliques in the team, and their prospects for the season were none too flattering.

But no matter how poorly a team had been going, they always seemed to brace up when they were to meet the Giants. They reserved their best pitchers for those games, and the fans came out in droves in order to see the proud team of the Metropolis humbled.

So the clean sweep that the Giants had been hoping for did not materialize. Markwith, to be sure, carried off the first game by a comfortable margin. He was one of the pitchers who when he was good was very good indeed, and on that day his southpaw slants were simply unhittable.

But the St. Louis evened things up the next day by beating Bradley, one of the Giants' second string pitchers, by a score of eight to five. On the following day, the pendulum swung again to the other side of the arc, and Jim chalked up a victory, despite some pretty free hitting by the home team.

The Giants pinned their hopes once again to Markwith in the last game of the series. He was not so good as on the opening day, but even then he might have won, had it not been for a stupid play by Iredell in the ninth inning.

One man was out in the Giants' last half. The score was seven to six in favor of St. Louis. Iredell had reached first on a single, and on a wild pitch had advanced to second. Burkett, the heavy hitting first baseman, was at the bat. A hit would probably bring Iredell in and tie the score.

Iredell was taking a pretty long lead off second and "Red" Smith, the Cardinal catcher, shot the ball down to second, hoping to catch him napping. Iredell, however, made a quick slide back to the bag and got there before Salberg, the Cardinal second baseman, could put the ball on him.

Iredell got up, grinned triumphantly at Salberg, dusted off his clothes, and again took a lead off the bag. Quick as a flash, Salberg, who had concealed the ball under his arm, ran up to Iredell and touched him out.

A groan of distress came from the Giants and their supporters and a roar of derision from the St. Louis crowd. That a big-league player could be caught by a trick that was as old as the hills seemed almost incredible. It was years since the moth-eaten play had been seen on a major-league diamond, and the crowd yelled itself hoarse.

Iredell stood for a moment as if stupefied, then he walked slowly into the bench, his face a flaming red. If McRae forebore to tell him what he thought of him, it was because he was so choked that the words would not come. But the glare that he turned on the luckless player was more eloquent than any words, even in his rich vocabulary.

Joe turned to Mabel, where he was sitting beside her in the stands immediately back of the pitcher.

"Did you see that?" he asked. "To think of a Giant player being caught by a sand-lot trick!"

"I didn't quite get it," answered Mabel. "I was looking at the batter at the time. Just what was it that happened?"

"Salberg hid the ball under his arm instead of throwing it back to the pitcher," explained Joe. "Iredell took it for granted that he had thrown it, and was so busy dusting off his clothes that he didn't make sure of it. Why, Shem tried that on Japhet when they came out of the ark. And to think that he chose this moment to pull that bonehead play! Look at that hit by Burkett. It would have brought Iredell home with the run which would have tied the score."

Their eyes followed the flight of the ball, which was a mighty three-bagger that Burkett had lined out between right and center. It brought a rousing cheer from the Giant partisans, and hope revived that the game might yet be saved. But the hope was vain, for the fly that Wheeler sent out into the field settled firmly in the leftfielder's hand, and the inning and the game were over, with the St. Louis having the big end of the score.

It was a hard game to lose, and it was a disgruntled lot of Giant players that filed off dejectedly to their dressing rooms. A sure tie, at least, had been within their grasp, and, as a matter of fact, a probable victory. For if Iredell had scored, as he could easily have done on the three base hit of Burkett, the latter would have been on third with only one man out instead of two and with the score tied. Then Wheeler's long hit, even though an out, would have gone for a sacrifice and Burkett could easily have scored from third, putting the Giants one run ahead. To be sure, the St. Louis would still have had the last half of the ninth, but the Giants, fighting to hold their advantage, would have had all the odds in their favor.

But all the post mortems in the world could not change the fact that the game had gone into the St. Louis column and that the Giants, instead of taking three out of four, had had to be content with an even break. It was small consolation that that was better than they had been able to do with the other Western teams. The trip had been a terrible flivver, one of the worst that the Giant team had ever made while swinging around the circle.

"That's the last straw that breaks the camel's back," growled McRae, savagely. "It'll make us the laughing stock of the League. Why, at thisminute, the crowds before the bulletin boards all over the United States are snickering at the Giants. Not merely a Giant player—that would be bad enough—but the Giant captain—get me?—the Giant captain, supposed to show his men how the game should be played, gets caught by the oldest and cheapest trick in the game. It's all we needed to wind up this trip. I want to go away somewhere and hide my head. I hate to go back and face the grins of the New York fans."

"It sure is tough," agreed Robbie. "Of course that finishes Iredell as captain."

"That goes without saying," replied McRae. "Even if I were disposed to overlook it and give him another chance, I couldn't do it now. When a captain, instead of being respected by his men, becomes the butt of the team and a joke to the fans all over the circuit, he's through."

A little later the stocky manager sought out Iredell and found him alone.

"I know what you want to see me about," Iredell forestalled him. "You want my resignation as captain of the team. Well, here it is," and he handed over a paper.

"All right, Iredell," returned McRae, after he had scanned the paper carefully and stowed it away in his pocket. "I'll accept this, and I won't say anything more about that play, because I know how sore you're feeling and I don't want to rub it in. I'll admit that at the time it happened, I saw red. But what's past is past, and there's no use crying about spilled milk."

"You can have my resignation as shortstop too, if you want it," growled Iredell, who was evidently in a nasty humor.

"I don't want it," said McRae, kindly. "You're a good shortstop, and I've no fault to find with your work as such. And now that you've got nothing to think about except playing your position, I hope you'll do better than ever. One thing I'm counting on, too, is that you cherish no grudges and give full loyalty to the man I'm going to make captain. Is that a go?"

Iredell grunted something that McRae chose to accept as an affirmative. But he would have changed his opinion if he had seen the ugly glare in Iredell's eyes and the clenched fist that Iredell shook at the manager's back as the latter walked away.

"Give me a dirty deal and expect me to take it lying down, do you?" he snarled. "You've got another guess coming, and don't you forget it!"

CHAPTER IX

THE NEW CAPTAIN

Although Iredell had himself offered his resignation, he had only done it to take the wind out of McRae's sails and put himself in a better strategic position. If worst came to worst, he could save his pride by saying that he had resigned of his own accord instead of being "fired."

But he had hoped, nevertheless, that the resignation would be refused and that McRae, after perhaps giving him a lecture, would accord him another chance. The prompt acceptance had caught him off his balance, and he was full of rage at the conviction that McRae had sought him out for the express purpose of displacing him.

As Robbie had previously intimated, Iredell was a poor sport. The events of the last few days should have taught him that the duties of captain were too much for him. But like many other people, he was inclined to blame everything and everybody else for his own shortcomings. He had been intensely vain of his position as captain of the team. His nature was, at bottom, petty and vindictive, and from the moment it dawned upon him what had happened to him, he framed a resolution to do all that lay in his power to thwart the plans of his successor. If he had failed, he would try to prove that whoever took his place could do no better.

With his resentment was mingled curiosity as to the man that was to succeed him. Who could it be? He ran over in his mind the other members of the outfield and infield, never once thinking of the pitchers, who were assumed to be out of the question. The more he pondered, the more puzzled he became. Well, after all, it did not matter. He would know soon enough. And whoever it was would find his work mighty hard for him, as far as he, Iredell, could make it so.

That night the Giants shook the dust of St. Louis from their feet, and with a sigh of relief, not unmingled with apprehension, took the train for the long jump home. Relief that the disastrous Western trip was at last over. Apprehension at the reception they would meet from the newspapers and fans of New York.

Mabel was to accompany Joe back to New York and remain there for about two weeks before she returned for a while to Goldsboro. Joe looked forward to these as golden days, and the outlook went far to console him for his chagrin at the Giants' poor showing.

His leg and foot were mending rapidly, and he hoped to be in form again almost as soon as he reached New York and to be able to go in and take his regular turn in the box. And if ever the Giants needed his pitching and batting strength, it was now!

He and Mabel had just returned from the dining car to the Pullman that first evening on the train that was bearing them East, when McRae and Robbie came along.

They knew Mabel well, because, on the trip of the Giants around the world, she had gone along with Mrs. McRae and other married women as chaperons.

"Blooming as a rose," said Robbie, gallantly. "When it comes to picking, we have to hand it to Joe."

"Still as full of blarney as ever," laughed Mabel. "I suppose you say that to every girl you meet."

"Not at all, not-at-all!" disclaimed Robbie, his round face beaming.

"King of Northern pitchers and queen of Southern women," put in McRae. "It's a winning combination."

"I'll admit the part about the women," agreed Joe.

"And I'll admit the part about the pitchers," said Mabel, her smile enhanced by a bewitching dimple.

"Then we're all happy," laughed McRae. "But now I'm going to ask the queen to let the king come along with Robbie and me into the smoking car for a while. I've got a little business to talk over."

"Hold on to me, Mabel," cried Joe, in mock alarm. "Mac wants to fire me, but he won't do it as long as I'm with you."

"I'm not very much worried," responded Mabel, merrily. "For that matter, I shouldn't wonder if you were honing to get rid of me. Go along now, and I'll console myself with a magazine until you get back."

The three men went into the smoking car and settled themselves comfortably. Then when the two older men had lighted cigars, McRae hurled a question.

"Joe, how would you like to be captain of the Giants?" he asked.

Joe was completely taken aback for a moment.

"Great Scott! You sure do hit a fellow right between the eyes, Mac," he responded. "Just what do you mean? You've got a captain now, haven't you?"

"I had an apology for a captain up to this afternoon," was the reply. "But I haven't even that now. Here, read this," and he thrust Iredell's written resignation into his hand.

Joe read it with minute attention.

"I'm sorry for Iredell," he remarked, as he refolded the paper and handed it back. "But I won't pretend that I'm surprised. But what strikes me all in a heap is your question to me. Remember that I'm a pitcher. As my brother-in-law, Reggie, would remark, 'it simply isn't done.'"

"You're a pitcher, all right," responded McRae, "and the best that comes. But you're more than that. You're a thinker. And that's the kind of man I've got to have for captain. There's no other man on the team that fills the bill. They'd rattle around in the position like a pea in a tincup. You'd fill it to perfection. That's the reason I offer it to you. You know, of course, that it means an increase in your salary, but I know that isn't the thing that would especially appeal to you. I want you to take the position because I think it will be the best thing for the Giants. Think it over."

There was silence for a few minutes while Joe thought it over and thought hard. He knew that it would mean an immense addition to his work and his responsibilities. He would have to play every day, while now he played, at the most, only twice a week.

Without self-conceit, he knew that he could qualify for the position. Again and again he had groaned inwardly at baseball sins of omission and commission that he felt sure would not have occurred had he had the deciding voice on the field.

It finally simmered down to this: Would it help the Giants? Would it increase their chances for the pennant? He decided that it would. And the moment he reached that conclusion his answer was ready.

"I'll take it, Mac," he announced.

"Bully!" exclaimed McRae, as he reached over and shook Joe's hand to bind the bargain. "Don't think for a minute, Joe, that I don't appreciate the immense amount of work that this will put upon you. I don't want to ride a willing horse to death."

"That's all right, Mac," answered Joe. "The only possible doubt in my mind was as to whether it might affect my pitching or hitting. I wouldn't want to let down in those things. But if you're willing to take a chance, I am."

"I'll take all the chances and all the responsibility," replied McRae, confidently. "I haven't watched you all these years for nothing. I've never asked you to do anything yet that you haven't done to the queen's taste. You've developed into the best pitcher in the game. You've developed into the best batter in the game. Now I look for you to develop into the best captain in the game."

"I'll bet dollars to doughnuts that he will," broke in Robbie, his rubicund face aglow with satisfaction. "Now we'll begin to see the Giants climb."

"I'm sure they will," affirmed McRae. "We've added fifty per cent. to the Giants' strength by this night's work. You know as well as I do, Joe, that the class is there. All it needs is to be brought out. And you're the boy that's going to do it. Put your fighting spirit into them. I was going to say put your brains into them, but that couldn't be done without a surgical operation. But you can teach them to use the brains they have, and that itself will go a long way."

"How did Iredell take it when you saw him?" asked Joe, thoughtfully.

"Of course he was sore," answered McRae. "But how much of that was due to his soreness over that bonehead play, and how much to the fact that I accepted his resignation so promptly, I can't say. But I don't think you'll have any trouble with him."

Joe, who knew Iredell's nature a good deal better than McRae, was not at all sure, but he said nothing.

"As for the other members of the team," went on McRae, "they all think you're about the best that ever happened, and I'm sure they'll be delighted with the change. You'll find them backing you up to the limit. The rookies, too, look up to you as a kingpin pitcher and batter, and they'll be just clay in your hands. You can do with them whatever you will. We've picked up some promising material there, and you're the one to bring out all that's in them."

"You can depend on me to do my best," Joe responded warmly.

"That means that we'll win the flag even with our bad beginning," declared McRae. "And now just one other thing, Joe. I want you to feel perfectly free to discuss with Robbie and me anything you think will be for the best interests of the team. If you think any man ought to be fired, tell me so. If you think of any player we can go out and get, tell me that, too. We'll welcome any suggestions. Have you anything of that kind now in mind? If so, let's have it."

"I certainly don't want any one fired," said Joe, with a smile. "At least, not for the present. As to getting any new players, I saw something in the evening papers a half an hour ago that set me thinking. Have you seen that the Yankees have determined to let Hays go?"

"No, I haven't," replied McRae with quickened interest. "I haven't looked at to-night's papers. But after all that won't do us any good. Some other club in the American League will snap him up."

"That's what I should have thought," answered Joe. "But the surprising thing is that all the other clubs in the American have waived claims upon him. That leaves us free to make an offer for him, if we want him."

"That's funny," mused McRae. "Remember the way he played against us in the World Series? He had us nailed to the mast and crying for help."

"He sure did," agreed Robbie. "But he hasn't been going very well since then. Rather hard to manage in the first place, and then, too, he seems to be losing his effectiveness. If no other club in the American League wants him, he must be nearly through."

"That's the way it struck me at first when I read the telegram," said Joe. "Then I got to thinking it over. Why don't the other clubs in the American League want him?"

"I'll bite," said McRae. "What's the answer?"

"Perhaps it's this," suggested Joe. "Hays, as you know, has that peculiar cross-fire delivery that singles him out among pitchers. No other pitcher in either League has one just like it. It isn't that it's so very effective when you come to know it. But because it's so unlike any other, it puzzles all teams until they get used to it. That's the way it was with us in the Series. The first two games we couldn't do a thing to him. In the third we were beginning to bat him more freely.

"Now, what does that lead up to? Just this. The other teams in the American League have become so used to his pitching that it's lost its terrors. If any one of them bought him from the Yankees, they'd have to stack him up against the seven other teams in their League who have learned to bat him without trouble.

"But with the National League it's different. It would take them considerable time to get on to him. In the meantime, he might have won two or three games from each of them before they solved him. He might be good for fifteen or twenty victories before this season is over. He might — —"

"By ginger!" interrupted McRae. "Joe, that think tank of yours is working day and night. I'll get in touch with the Yankee management by wire at the next station."

CHAPTER X

GETTING IN SHAPE

"There's something right off the bat for a starter," exulted Robbie. "Now, how about the rest of the team?"

"I think they're just about as good as they come," remarked Joe. "Jackwell and Bowen are a big improvement on Hupft and McCarney both in fielding and batting. Burkett is digging them out of the dirt at first all right, and Larry takes everything that comes into his territory. Our outfield is one of the heaviest hitting in the League — —"

"And it will hit harder yet when you're playing out there the days you're not in the box," chuckled Robbie. "They'll have to move back the fences in the ball parks for your homers. You'll break up many a game with that old wagon spoke of yours."

"Oh, the days I play in the outfield, one of the men will have to be benched," mused Joe. "Which one shall it be?"

"We'll let that depend on the way they keep up with the stick," said McRae. "That will be a spur to them. Neither Curry nor Wheeler nor Bowen will want to sit on the bench, and they'll work their heads off to keep on the batting order. There again it will be a good thing for the team. Every man will be fighting to make the best showing possible."

"Talking about Jackwell and Bowen," remarked Robbie. "Have you ever noticed anything queer about those birds?"

"They don't seem to be as husky as they might be," observed McRae. "Just the other day they begged to be let off because they said they were sick. Over eating, perhaps. That's a common fault with young players when they first come into the big League and eat at the swell hotels."

"It wasn't that I meant," explained Robbie. "They seem to be nervous and jumpy. Looking around as though they expected every minute to feel somebody's hand on their shoulder."

"I've noticed that," said Joe. "It was only the other day I was speaking to Jim about it. Probably it will wear off when they get a little better used to big-league company. I'll have a quiet little talk with them about it."

For another hour they discussed matters bearing on the welfare of the club, and then Joe went back to Mabel.

"I thought you'd forgotten all about poor little me," she said, with an adorable pout of her pretty lips.

Joe looked around to see that no one was observing them, and straightened out the pout in a manner perfectly satisfactory to both.

"Well, did McRae fire you, as you call it?" asked Mabel.

"Hardly," answered Joe, as he settled himself beside her. "In fact, instead of kicking me downstairs he kicked me up."

"Meaning?" said Mabel, with a questioning intonation.

"Meaning," repeated Joe, "that he made me captain of the Giant team."

"What!" exclaimed Mabel, as though she could not believe her ears.

"Just that," was the reply.

"Oh, Joe, what an honor!" exclaimed Mabel, with pride and delight. "I'm so proud! That's another proof of what they think of you."

"I suppose it is an honor," agreed Joe, "and it will mean a nice little addition to my salary. I'll clean up over twenty thousand this year altogether. And, if we get into the World Series, there will be a few thousands more. But it means a great addition of work and responsibility."

"You mustn't overtax yourself, dear," said Mabel, anxiously. "Remember that your health and strength are above everything."

"If I felt any healthier or stronger than I am now, I'd be afraid of myself," replied Joe, grinning. "Don't worry, honey. All I care for is to make good in my new job."

"You'll do that," said Mabel, proudly, as she patted his hand. "You'd make good in anything. You'd make a good president of the United States."

"I'd be sure of one vote, anyhow, if I ran for the presidency," laughed Joe. "In fact, I'm afraid they'd have you pinched for repeating. You'd try to stuff the ballot boxes."

The long journey ended at last, with all the players glad to be back in what they fondly referred to as "little old New York." There was no brass band to meet them at the station, nor had the fans turned out in any great numbers, as they did when the Giants returned from a triumphant trip. It was an unusual experience for the Giants, who had the reputation of a great road team and commonly arrived with scalps at their belt. At present, however, they were distinctly out of favor. Nor did they derive any comfort from the brief and sarcastic references to their return in the columns of the city press.

Joe and Mabel took a taxicab to the hotel where they usually made their headquarters. Reggie, to his regret, had not been able to accompany them, though he promised to come on later.

"Beastly shame," he had said, in parting, "that I could only see the Giants when they were coming a cropper. But I'll get to the big city soon and see them get even with those rotters. My word! It's been simply disgustin'!"

The perfect rest during the journey had been of immense benefit to Joe's injured leg and foot, and he was overjoyed to find that he was now as fit as ever. The perfect physical condition in which he kept himself had contributed toward a quick recovery.

The relief and satisfaction of McRae and Robbie over his condition were unbounded, for with Joe out of the game the Giants were a different and far inferior team.

Mabel had plenty of shopping and sightseeing to keep her spare time employed through the day, and at night she and Joe had a delightful time taking in the best shows on Broadway.

The first morning that the team turned out for practice on the Polo Grounds, Joe sought an opportunity for a quiet talk with Iredell.

The fact that McRae had made a generous interpretation of the clause in Iredell's contract regarding his salary as captain had not abated the resentment of that individual. He had been moody and grouchy ever since his displacement, and had nursed his supposed grievance until his heart was fairly festering with bitterness. He was sore at McRae, but even more so at Joe, as his successor. The latter, he persuaded himself, had intrigued to get his place.

"I'm going to have a talk with all the boys together, Iredell," Joe greeted him pleasantly, in a secluded corner of the grounds. "But first I wanted to see you personally. I just want to say that we've always got along together all right, that I value you as one of the best players on the team, and that I hope our pleasant relations will continue."

But Iredell was in no mood to take the olive branch that Joe held out to him.

"I suppose I'll have to do what you tell me to," he muttered sourly. "You're the boss now."

"I don't like that word 'boss,'" returned Joe. "I don't have any of the feeling that that word implies. If I have to exercise the authority that has been given me, it will be simply because that's my job, and not because I have a swelled head. McRae's the boss of all of us. You say you'll have to do what I tell you to. But I'm hoping you'll do your best, not because I tell you to, but because you want to do whatever is for the best interests of the team. How about it, Iredell? Does that go?"

"Oh, what's the use of talking about it," snapped Iredell. "I'll do my work as shortstop. You've got the job you've been working for. Let it go at that."

His tone was so offensive, to say nothing of the implication of his words, that Joe had to make a mighty effort to restrain his naturally quick temper. But he knew that he could not rule others unless he had first learned to master himself. So that it was with no trace of anger that he replied:

"Listen to me, Iredell. I haven't worked for this job. I didn't want it. I hadn't even thought of it. I was struck all in a heap when McRae asked me to take it. And at that time, you'd already resigned. That's the absolute truth."

Iredell made no answer, but his sniff of unbelief spoke volumes. Joe saw that while he was in this mood there was nothing to be gained by talking longer.

"Think it over, old boy," he said pleasantly. "I'm your friend, and I want to stay your friend. I know how well you can play, and I'm sure you're going to do your best with the rest of us to bring the pennant once more to New York."

He moved away, and a little later had gathered the rest of the team in the clubhouse.

"I'm not going to do much talking, fellows," he said. "McRae has already told you that I'm to be captain of the team. I'm proud to be captain of such a bunch. I feel that all of us are brothers. We've been comrades in many a hard fight, and there are lots of such fights ahead of us. But all our fighting will be done against the other fellows and not among ourselves. I'm counting on every one of you to go in and work his head off for the good of the team. That must be the only thing that counts with any of us.

"I don't want to exercise a single bit of authority that I don't have to. But I'm not going to fall down on my job if I can help it. If I have to call a man down, I'll call him down. While we're out on the field, what I say will have to go. You may think it's right or you may think it's rotten, but all the same it will have to go. But you'll understand that there's nothing personal and that whatever's done is for the good of the team. You know I'd rather boost than roast, and that I'll praise a good play just as readily as I'd blame a bad one. Now how about it, fellows? Are you with me?"

"We're wid ye till the cows come home!" shouted Larry, enthusiastically. "Three cheers for the new captain!"

Rousing cheers shook the clubhouse and sealed the compact.

Then, with a new spirit, the Giants plunged into the pennant fight. It was a hard fight that lay before them, and none of them underrated it. But the grim determination that had been in evidence many times previously was now again to the fore, and it boded ill for their rivals.

Mabel, after a tender parting, had returned for a brief while to Goldsboro, and Joe concentrated all the energies of brain and body on his new task. Like the war horse, he "sniffed the battle from afar," and was eager to plunge into the thick of the fray. Would he emerge the winner?

Baseball Joe, for the time being, gave no more attention to Iredell's grouchiness. He knew the player felt sore, but never realized how far that soreness might carry the fellow.

"I'll fix him some day, see if I don't," muttered Iredell to himself when on his way to the hotel that night. "I'll fix him. Just wait and see! I'll teach him to ride over me!"

CHAPTER XI

WINGING THEM OVER

"So 'tis your birthday, I do be hearin', Joe," remarked Larry Barrett, the jovial second baseman of the team, as the Giants were getting into their uniforms preparatory to going out on the field.

"That's what," laughed Joe, as he finished tying his shoe laces.

"I'll bet you were a ball player from the cradle," grinned Larry.

"I guess I bawled all right," Joe replied. "And once, my mother tells me, I pitched headlong from my baby carriage."

"What would you like for a birthday present?" queried Wheeler.

"Ten runs," replied Joe, promptly. "Give me those to-day and I won't ask for anything else."

"Pretty big order," remarked Wheeler, dubiously. "Ten runs are a lot to make against those Brooklyn birds. I hear they're going to put in Dizzy Rance to-day, and he's a lulu. Won his last eight games and has started in to make a record. Have a heart, Joe, and make it five."

"Five's plenty," asserted Jim, confidently. "I'm willing to bet that's more than the Dodgers will get, with Joe in the box."

"We'll know more about that when the game's over," said Joe, as he moved toward the door.

"Gee! Look at those stands and bleachers," remarked Jim, as he and his chum came out on the field. "Seems as though all New York and Brooklyn had turned out. And it's nearly an hour before the game begins. They'll be turning them away from the gates."

"Almost like a World Series crowd," agreed Joe, as they made their way across the green velvet turf of the outfield toward the Giants' dugout.

It was a phenomenal throng for that stage of the playing season, and was accounted for by the traditional rivalry between the two teams, which, while hailing from different boroughs, were both included within the limits of Greater New York. They fought each other like Kilkenny cats whenever they came together. No matter how indifferently they might have been going with other teams, they always braced when they had each other as opponents. It was not an uncommon thing, even in the seasons when the Giants had taken the series from every other team in the League, to lose the majority of the games with the Brooklyns, even though the latter might be tagging along in the rear of the second division.

But this year the Brooklyns were going strong, and it was generally admitted that they had a look-in for the pennant. Several trades during the previous winter had strengthened the weak places in the line-up, and their pitching staff was recognized as one of the best in either League.

"Going to pick the feathers off those birds to-day, Joe?" asked McRae, as Joe came up to the Giants' bench, where the manager was sitting.

"I sure am going to try," replied Joe. "It's about time we put a crimp in their winning streak."

Joe beckoned to Mylert, and they went out to warm up. He was feeling in excellent fettle, and he soon found that he had all his "stuff" with him. His curve had a sharp break, his slow ball floated up so that it seemed to be drifting, and his fast ones whizzed over like a bullet.

"You've got the goods to-day, Joe," pronounced Mylert, and he fairly winced at the way the ball shot into his hands. "You've got speed to burn. Those balls just smoke. With that control of yours you could hit a coin. They can't touch you. They'll be rolling over and playing dead."

"That listens good," laughed Joe. "At that, I'll need all I've got to make those fellows be good."

The preliminary practice gave evidence that the game would be for blood. Both teams were on their toes, and the dazzling plays that featured their work brought frequent roars of applause from the Giant and Brooklyn rooters. Then the bell rang, the umpire dusted off the plate and the vast throng settled down with delighted anticipation to watch the game.

The Brooklyns, as the visiting team, went first to bat. A roar went up from the stands as Joe walked out to the mound. The Giant rooters promptly put the game down as won. But the Brooklyns pinned their faith to their phenomenal pitcher, Dizzy Rance, and had different ideas about the outcome of the game.

The first inning was short and sweet. Leete, the leftfielder of the Dodgers, who, year in and year out, had a batting average of .300 or better, swung savagely at the first ball pitched and raised a skyscraping fly that Jackwell at third promptly gathered in. Mornier, with the count at three balls and two strikes, sent up a foul that Mylert caught close to the stands after a long run. Tonsten lunged at the first ball and missed. The second was a beauty that cut the outer corner of the plate at which he did not offer and which went for a strike. Then Joe shot over a high fast one and struck him out.

"Atta boy, Joe!" and similar shouts of encouragement came from stands and bleachers, as Joe pulled off his glove and went in to the bench.

Rance, the Brooklyn pitcher, did not lack a generous round of applause as he took up his position in the box. He had already pitched two games against the Giants and won them both. But he had never happened to be pitted against Joe, and despite his air of confidence he knew he had his work cut out for him.

Curry made a good try on the second ball pitched and sent a long fly to center that was caught by Maley after a long run. Iredell sent a sharp single to left. Burkett slammed one off Rance's shins, and the ball rolled between short and second. Before it could be recovered, Burkett had reached first and Iredell was safe at second. Wheeler tried to wait Rance out, but when the count had reached three and two he sent a single to center that scored Iredell from second and carried Burkett to third. A moment later the latter was caught napping by a snap throw from catcher to third and came in sheepishly to the bench. Rance then put on steam and set Jackwell down on three successive strikes.

"There's one of the runs we promised you, Joe," sang out Larry, as the Giants took the field.

"That's good as far as it goes," laughed Joe. "But don't forget I'm looking for more."

For the Brooklyns, Trench was an easy out on a roller to Joe, who ran over and tagged him on the base line. Naylor dribbled one to Jackwell that rolled so slowly that the batter reached first. But no damage was done, for Joe pitched an outcurve to Maley and made him hit into a fast double play, Iredell to Barrett to Burkett.

It was snappy pitching, backed up by good support, and that it was appreciated was shown by the shouts that came from the Giant rooters, who cheered until Joe had to remove his cap.

But Rance, although the Giants had got to him for three hits in the first inning, showed strength in the second that delighted his supporters. He mowed the Giants down as fast as they came to the bat.

The best that Larry could do was to lift a towering fly to center that was taken care of by Maley. Bowen lifted a twisting foul that the Brooklyn catcher did not have to stir out of his tracks to get. Joe hit a smoking liner that was superbly caught by Tonsten, who had to go up in the air for it, but held on.

In the Brooklyns' third, Joe made a great play on a well-placed bunt by Reis that rolled between the box and third base. Joe slipped and fell as he grasped it, but while in a sitting position he shot it over to first in time to nail the runner. Rance hit a sharp bounder to the box that Joe fielded in plenty of time. Tighe went out on a Texas leaguer that was gathered in by Larry.

"That boy's got 'em eating out of his hand," exulted Robbie, his red face beaming with satisfaction.

"Yes, now," agreed the more cautious McRae. "But at any time they may turn and bite the hand that's feeding them. They're an ungrateful lot."

In their half of the inning, the Giants failed to score. Rance was pitching like a house afire. Mylert went back to the bench after three futile offers at the elusive sphere. Curry popped a weak fly to Trench, and, Iredell, after fouling the ball off half a dozen times, grounded to Mornier at first, who only had to step on the bag to register an out.

It was Larry's turn to be in the limelight in the Brooklyns' half of the fourth. Leete raised a fly that seemed destined to fall between second and left. It was certain that Wheeler at left could not get to it in time, though he came in racing like an express train. But Larry had started at the crack of the bat, running in the direction of the ball. He reached it just as it was going over his head, and with a wild leap grasped it with one hand and held on to it.

It was one of the finest catches ever made on the Polo Grounds. For a moment the crowd sat stupefied. Then, when they realized that a baseball"miracle" had occurred, they raised a din that could have been heard a mile away.

"Great stuff, Larry, old boy!" congratulated Joe, as the second baseman resumed his position. "No pitcher could ask for any better support than that."

"Let that go for my share of your birthday present," returned the grinning Larry.

The next two went out in jig time, one on a grounder and the other on strikes.

The Giants added one more run in their half of the fourth by a clever combination of bunts and singles. Joe knew that Rance was weak on fielding bunts, and he directed his men to play on that weakness. The Brooklyn pitcher fell all over himself in trying to handle them, and this had a double advantage, for it not only let men get on bases but it shook for a moment the morale of the boxman and made it easier for the succeeding batsman. It was only by virtue of a lucky double play that Rance got by with only one run scored against him in that inning.

With two runs to the good, the Giants went out on the field in a cheerful mood. They were getting onto the redoubtable Rance, not heavily, but still they were hitting him. Joe, on the other hand, seemed to be invincible. He was not trying for strike-outs except when necessary. But his curves were working perfectly, his control was marvelous, and when a third strike was in order he called upon his hop ball or his fadeaway and it did the trick.

And the boys behind him were certainly backing him up in fine style. They were fairly "eating up" everything that came their way, digging them out of the dirt, spearing them out of the air, throwing with the precision of expert riflemen. None of them was playing that day for records. They were playing for the team. Already the new spirit that Joe had infused as captain was beginning to tell.

In the Giant's half of the fifth, Joe was the first man up. Rance tried him on an outcurve, but Joe refused to bite. The next was a fast, straight one, and Joe caught it fairly for a terrific smash over the centerfielder's head. The outfield had gone back when he first came to the bat, but they had not gone back far enough. It was a whale of a hit, and Joe trotted home easily, even then reaching the plate before Maley had laid his hand on the ball.

"Frozen hoptoads!" cried Robbie, fairly jumping up and down in exultation. "It's a murderer he is. He isn't satisfied with anything less than killing the ball."

"He's some killer, all right," assented McRae. "With one other man like him on the team, the race would be over. The Giants would simply walk in with the flag."

That mammoth hit should have been the beginning of a rally, but Rance tightened up and the next three went out in order, one on strikes and the other two on infield outs.

Joe still had control of the situation, and he seemed to grow more unhittable as the game went on. He simply toyed with his opponents, and their vain attempts to land on the ball made them at times seem ludicrous.

"Sure, Joe, 'tis a shame what you're doin' to those poor boobs," chuckled Larry, as they came in to the bench together.

"But don't forget that they're always dangerous," cautioned Joe. "Do you remember the fourteen runs they made in one of their games against the Phillies? They may stage a comeback any minute."

"Not while you're in the box, old boy," declared Larry. "You'll have to break a leg to lose this game."

Burkett thought it was up to him to do something, and lammed out a terrific liner to left for three bases, sliding into third just a fraction of a second before the return of the ball. Wheeler tried to sacrifice, but Tonsten held Burkett at third by a threatening gesture before putting out Wheeler at first. With the infield pulled in for a play at the plate, Jackwell double-crossed them by a single over short that scored Burkett with the fourth run for the Giants. Barrett went out on a grounder to Mornier, Jackwell taking second. Bowen made a determined effort to bring him in, but his long fly to center was gathered in by Maley.

The "lucky seventh" was misnamed as far as the Brooklyns were concerned, for their luck was conspicuous by its absence. Although the heavy end of their batting order was up, they failed to get the ball out of the infield. Leete, their chief slugger, was utterly bewildered by Joe's offerings and struck out among the jeers of the Giant fans. Mornier popped up a fly that Joe gobbled up, and Larry had no trouble in getting Tonsten's grounder into the waiting hands of Burkett.

The Giants did a little better, and yet were unable to add to their score. Joe started off with a ripping single to left. Mylert tried to advance him by sacrificing, but after sending up two fouls was struck out by Rance. Curry sent a liner to the box that was too hot to handle, but Rance deflected it to Tonsten who got Curry at first, Joe in the meantime getting to second. Iredell was an easy victim, driving the ball straight into the hands of Mornier at first.

"Well, Joe," chuckled Jim, as the eighth inning began, "we haven't given you your present yet, but we're in a fair way to put it over. Not to say that you're not earning most of the present yourself."

"I don't care how it comes as long as we get it," laughed Joe, as he slipped on his glove.

The time was now growing fearfully short in which the men from the other side of the bridge could make their final bid for the game. Those four runs that the Giants had scored were like so many mountains to be scaled, and with the airtight pitching that Joe was handing out, it seemed like an impossible task.

Still, they had pulled many a game out of the fire with even greater odds against them, and they came up to the plate determined to do it again, if it were at all possible.

Trench got a ball just where he liked it, and sent it whistling to left field for a single. Naylor followed with a fierce grasser that Iredell knocked down, but could not field in time to catch the runner. It looked like the beginning of a rally, and the Brooklyn bench was in commotion. Their coaches on the base lines jumped up and down, alternately shouting encouragement to their men and hurling gibes at Joe in the attempt to rattle him.

"We've got him going now," yelled one.

"We've just been kidding him along so far," shouted another. "All together now, boys! Send him to the showers!"

Maley came next, with orders to strike at the first ball pitched. He followed orders and missed. Again he swung several inches under Joe's throw, which took a most tantalizing hop just before it reached the plate.

He set himself for the third and caught it fairly. The ball started as a screaming liner, going straight for the box. Joe leaped in the air and caught it in his gloved hand. Like a flash he turned and hurled it to Larry at second. Trench, who had started for third at the crack of the ball, tried frantically to scramble back to second, but was too late.

Larry wheeled and shot down the ball to first, beating Naylor to the bag by an eyelash. Three men had been put out in the twinkling of an eye!

It was the first triple play that had been made that season, and the third that had been made on the Polo Grounds since that famous park had been opened. It had all occurred so quickly that half the spectators did not for the moment realize what had occurred. But they woke up, and roar after roar rose from the stands as the spectators saw the Giants running in gleefully, while the discomfited Brooklyns, with their rally nipped in the bud, went out gloomily to their positions.

"You'll send him to the showers, will you?" yelled Larry to the Brooklyn coaches, as he threw his cap hilariously into the air.

Rance's face was a study as he took his place in the box. He saw his winning streak going glimmering. It was a hard game for him to lose, for he had pitched in a way that would have won most games. But he had drawn a hard assignment in having to face pitching against which his teammates, fence breakers as they usually were, could make no headway.

Still, he was game, and there was still another inning, and nothing was impossible in baseball. If the Giants had expected him to crack, they were quickly undeceived. Burkett grounded out to Trench, who made a rattling stop and got him at first with feet to spare. Wheeler fouled out to Tighe. Jackwell went out on three successive strikes.

It was a plucky exhibition of pitching under discouraging conditions, and Rance well deserved the hand that he received as he went in to the bench.

"I say, Joe," remarked Jim, as his chum was preparing to go out for the ninth Brooklyn inning. "Celebrate your birthday by showing those birds the three-men-to-a-game stunt. It will be a glorious wind-up."

"I'll see," replied Joe, with a grin that was half a promise.

Thompson, the manager of the Brooklyns, who had been having a little run-in with the umpire, and was standing in a disgruntled mood near the batter's box, overheard the dialogue and stared in wonderment at Jim.

"What's that three-men-to-a-game stunt you're talking about?" he asked.

"Haven't you ever heard of it?" asked Jim.

"I never have," replied Thompson. "And I was in the game before you were born."

"Then you've got a treat in store for you," Jim assured him. "Just you watch this inning, and you'll see that only three men will be needed to turn your men back without a run, or even the smell of a hit. They'll be the pitcher, the catcher and the first baseman. The rest of the Giants will have nothing to do and might as well be off the field. In fact, if it wasn't against the regulations of the game, we would call them into the bench just now."

Thompson looked at Jim as though he were crazy.

"Trying to kid me?" the Brooklyn manager asked, with a savage inflection in his voice.

"Not at all," replied Jim, grinning cheerfully. "Just keep your eye on that pitcher of ours."

CHAPTER XII

AN AMAZING FEAT

Thompson, still believing that Jim was trying to get a rise out of him, walked back to his own bench, growling to himself.

Reis was the first to face Joe in the last half of the ninth. Joe measured him carefully, took his time in winding up, and then, with all the signs of delivering a fast high one, sent over a floater that Reis reached for and hit into the dirt in front of the plate. Joe ran on it, picked it up and tossed it to Burkett for an easy out.

Rance, the Brooklyn pitcher, came to the plate. Joe sent over a hop that Rance caught on the under side for a foul high up back of the rubber that Mylert caught without moving from his position.

With two out, Tighe missed the first one that came over so fast that it had settled in Mylert's glove before the batter had completed his swing. The next he fouled off for strike two. Then Joe whizzed over his old reliable fadeaway.

"You're out!" cried the umpire.

The game was over and the Giants had beaten their redoubtable foes by a score of four to none. They had whitewashed their opponents and broken their winning streak.

And what was sweeter to Jim at the moment was that Joe had fulfilled his prediction. Only the pitcher, catcher and first baseman had been necessary to turn the Brooklyns back. The other six men of the Giant team had had nothing to do and might as well have been off the field. It was almost magical pitching, the climax of the art.

Joe and Jim grinned at each other in a knowing way as the former came into the bench.

"You pulled it off that time all right, Joe!" exclaimed Jim gleefully, as he threw his arm around his chum's shoulder. "I piped off Thompson to what you were going to do and he thought I had gone nutty. He'd have given me an awful razz if it had failed to go through."

"You were taking awful chances," laughed Joe. "Of course, I might do that once in a while, but only a superman could do it all the time. But in this inning, luck was with us."

Thompson at this moment came strolling over toward them. He was evidently consumed with curiosity.

"I'll take the wind out of your sails at the start by admitting that you put one over on me," he said, addressing himself to Jim. "Though how you knew what was about to happen is beyond me. How did you do it?" he asked, turning to Joe. "Have you got a horseshoe or rabbit's foot concealed about you?"

"I assure you that I have nothing up my sleeve to deceive you," Joe said, rolling up his sleeves in the best manner of the professional conjurer. "It simply means that the hand is quicker than the eye."

"Cut out the funny stuff and tell me just how you did it," persisted Thompson.

"I'll tell you," said McRae, who had been an amused listener to the conversation. "That's an old trick of Joe's that he's tried out when we've been playing exhibition games in the spring training practice. More than once, we've called in the whole team, except Joe, the catcher, and the first baseman. Then Joe's done just what he did this afternoon. Of course, it doesn't always go through, but in many cases he has put it over."

"There isn't another pitcher in the League who would dare try it!" exclaimed Thompson.

"There's only one Matson in the world," said McRae simply. "On the level, Thompson, what would you give to have him on your team?"

"A quarter of a million dollars," blurted out Thompson.

"You couldn't have him for half a million," said McRae, with a grin, as he turned away.

It was a jubilant crowd of Giants that gathered in the clubhouse after the game.

"How was that for your birthday present, Joe?" sang out Larry. "It wasn't quite what you asked for, but it was the best we could do."

"It was plenty," laughed Joe. "I'd rather have those runs you gave me than a diamond ring. Keep it up, boys, and we'll soon be up at the top of the League. We've been a long time in getting started, but now just watch our smoke. This game pulls us out of the second division. We're right on the heels of the Brooklyns. Let's give those fellows to-morrow the same dose they got to-day. Then we'll get after the Pittsburghs and the Chicagos."

"That's the stuff!" cried Larry. "We'll show 'em where they get off. They've been hogging the best seats in this show. Now we'll send 'em back to the gallery."

Joe smiled happily at the enthusiasm of the boys. It was what he had been trying to instill ever since he had been made the captain of the team. He knew that the material was there—the batting, the fielding, and the pitching. But all this counted for nothing as long as the spirit was lacking, the will to victory, the confidence that they could win.

There was just one piece of the machinery, however, that was not working smoothly, and that was Iredell. He had been sulky and mutinous ever since he had been displaced by Joe in the captaincy of the team. Joe had been most considerate and had gone out of his way to be kind to him, but all his advances had been rebuffed.

"You're certainly getting the team into fine shape, Joe," said Jim, as they made their way out of the grounds. "They played championship ball behind you this afternoon."

"They sure did," agreed Joe. "Those plays by Larry, especially, were sparklers. I never saw the old boy in better form. He's one of the veterans of the game, and you might expect him to be slipping, but to-day he played like a youngster with all a veteran's skill. If everybody had the same spirit, I'd have nothing more to ask."

"Meaning Iredell, I suppose," said Jim.

"Just him," replied Joe. "It isn't that there's anything especially I can lay my hands on. He plays good mechanical ball. His fielding is good and he's keeping up fairly well with the stick. But the mischief of it is, it's all mechanical. He's like a galvanized dead man going through the motions, but a dead man just the same. I wish I could put some life into him. After a while, that dulness of his will begin to affect the rest of the team. It takes only one drop of ink to darken a whole glass of water."

"I noticed that in the clubhouse this afternoon," said Jim thoughtfully, "all the rest of the fellows were bubbling over, while he sat apart with a frown on his face as though we'd lost the game instead of having won it."

"Well, he'll have to get over that and get over it quickly," said Joe with decision. "We can't have him casting a wet blanket over the rest of the team. The trouble is, we haven't any one available to put in his place just now, and it's hard to get one at this stage of the season. Renton's a likely youngster, but he needs a little more seasoning before I could trust him in such a responsible position as that of shortstop."

"If that Mornsby deal had only gone through, we'd have had a crackerjack," said Jim regretfully.

"We sure would!" replied Joe. "But I felt from the beginning that we didn't have much chance of getting him. If the St. Louis management had let him go, they might as well have shut up shop. The fans would have hooted them out of town. Anyway, I'd rather develop a player than buy him. I'm going to coach young Renton with a possible view to taking Iredell's place, if it becomes necessary."

The next day Brooklyn again came to the Polo Grounds, determined to regain their lost laurels of the day before. This time they relied on Reuter, while McRae sent Jim into the box.

That Reuter was good, became evident before the game had gone very far. He had a world of speed and his curves were breaking well. Up to the seventh inning, only two hits had been made off of him, one of which was a homer by Joe and another a two-base hit by Burkett. His support was superb, and more than one apparent hit was turned into an out by clever fielding.

Jim, in the early innings, was not up to his usual mark. He had most of the stuff that had given him such high repute as a pitcher, except that he could not handle his wide-breaking curve with his usual skill. The failure of that curve to break over the plate got him several times in the hole. He relied too much also on his slow ball when, with the dull, cloudy weather that prevailed, speed would have been more effective.

But, although he was not in his best form, his courage never faltered. He was game in the pinches. Leete, for instance, in the fifth inning, laced the first ball pitched into leftfield for a clean homer. There was no one out when the mighty clout was made, but Jim refused to be disconcerted. He struck out Mornier, the heavy hitting first baseman of the Dodgers, made Tonsten hit a slow roller to the box that went for an easy out, and fanned Trench, after the latter had sent up two fouls in his unavailing attempt to hit the ball squarely.

Again in the sixth, after a triple and a single in succession had scored another run, he settled down and mowed the next three down in order.

But though his nerve was with him, the Brooklyn batsmen kept getting to him, picking up one run after the other until at the end of the seventh inning they had four runs to their credit while only one lone score had been made by the Giants. The Brooklyn rooters were jubilant, for it looked as though their pets had just about sewed up the game.

But in the Giants' half of the eighth Reuter began to crack. He started well enough by making Curry pop to Mornier. Iredell came next and shot a single to left, his first hit of the game and the third that had been made off Reuter up to that time. Then Burkett followed suit with a beauty to right that sent Iredell to third, though a good return throw by Reis held Burkett to the initial bag.

The two hits in succession seemed to affect Reuter's control, and he gave Wheeler a base on balls. Now the bags were full, with only one man out, and the Giant rooters, who had hitherto been glum, were standing up in their places and shouting like mad.

McRae sent Ledwith, a much faster man than Wheeler, to take the latter's place on first, while he himself ran out on the coaching line and Robbie scurried in the direction of third.

Jackwell was next at bat, and the chances were good for a double play by Brooklyn. But Reuter's tired arm had lost its cunning and, try as he would, he could not get the ball over the plate. Amid a pandemonium of yells from the excited fans he passed Jackwell to first, forcing a run over the plate. And still the bases were full.

It was evident that Reuter was "through," and Thompson signaled him to come in. He took off his glove and walked into the bench to a chorus of sympathetic cheers from the partisans of both sides in recognition of the superb work he had done up to that fateful inning.

Grimm took his place and tossed a few balls to the catcher in order to warm up. It was a hard assignment to take up the pitcher's burden with the bases full.

The first ball he put over came so near to "beaning" Larry that the latter only saved himself by dropping to the ground. McRae signaled to him to wait the pitcher out. He did so, with the result that he, too, trotted to first on four bad balls, forcing another run home and making the score four to three in favor of the Brooklyns.

Grimm braced for the next man, Bowen, and struck him out, as Bowen let even good balls go by, hoping to profit by the pitcher's wildness. But this time he reckoned without his host and retired discomfited to the bench.

Joe came next and received a mighty hand as he went to the plate. His three comrades on the bases implored him to bring them home.

Grimm was in a dilemma. Under ordinary circumstances he would have passed Joe and taken a chance on Mylert. But to pass him now meant the forcing home of another run, which would have tied the score. On the other hand, a clean hit would bring at least two men home and put the Giants ahead. There was still, however, the third chance—that Joe might not make a hit. In that case there would be three men out, leaving the Brooklyns ahead.

He took the third alternative and pitched to Joe, putting all the stuff he had on the ball. Joe swung at it and missed. Two balls followed in succession. Then he whizzed over a high, fast one that Joe caught fairly and sent out on a line between left and center for a sizzling triple, clearing the bases and himself coming into third standing up.

The Giants and their partisans went wild with joy as the three men followed each over the plate, making the score six to four in favor of the home team.

And at that figure the score remained, for Jim pitched like a man possessed in the Brooklyn's half of the ninth and set them down as fast as they came to the bat.

"That's what you call pulling the game out of the fire," exulted Larry, as the Giants were holding a jubilee in the clubhouse after the game.

"Yes," agreed Jim. "But it was a hard game for Reuter to lose. He outpitched me up to that fatal eighth inning. He had a world of stuff on the ball."

"He's a crackerjack, all right," agreed Joe. "And it certainly looked as though he had us going."

"Didn't have you going much that I could notice, except going around the bases," declared Larry, with a wide grin. "That was a corking homer of yours, and the triple was almost as good."

"Better, as far as the results were concerned," put in Jim. "For it brought home three men and settled the game. It was a life saver, and no mistake. Talk about Johnny on the spot. Joe on the spot is the salvation of the Giants!"

CHAPTER XIII
CLEVER STRATEGY

"Quit your kidding," laughed Joe. "Let's just say that the breaks of the game were with us and let it go at that. The main thing is that we've put another game on the right side of the ledger. We've turned the Brooklyns back, and now it's up to us to give the same dose to the Bostons and the Phillies."

"They'll be easy," prophesied Curry, as he finished fastening his shoe laces.

"Don't fool yourself," cautioned Joe. "They're playing better now than they were earlier in the season, and they won't be such cinches as they were in the last series. We'll have to step lively to beat them, and keep trying every minute. Ginger's the word from now on."

"Ginger" had been his watchword ever since he had been made captain of the team. He had tried to inspire them with his own indomitable energy and vim, and was gratified to see that with the exception of Iredell he was succeeding. It was doubly necessary in the case of the Giants, for most of the team was composed of veterans. They were superb players, but some of them were letting up on their speed and needed prodding to keep them at the top of their form.

Still there had been an infusion of new blood, and McRae was constantly on the lookout for more. The Giants' roster contained a number of promising rookies, such as Renton, Ledwith, Merton and others, and Joe was constantly coaching them in the fine points of the game.

In Merton, especially, he thought he had all the material of a promising pitcher. The youngster had been obtained from the Oakland Seals, and had won a high reputation in the Pacific Coast League. He had speed, a good assortment of curves, and a fair measure of control. But pitching against big leaguers was a very different matter from trying to outguess minor league batters, and Joe had not thought it advisable as yet to send him in for a full game.

One of his chief faults was that opponents could steal bases on him with comparative impunity. It was almost uncanny to note the ease with which a runner on the bases could detect whether Merton was going to pitch to the batter or throw the ball to first. Joe was not long in discovering the reason.

"Here's your trouble, Merton," he said. "You invariably lift your right heel from the ground when you are about to throw to the plate. You keep it on the ground when you're planning to throw to first. So, by watching you, those fellows can get a long lead off first and easily make second. Just try now, and see."

"You're right," admitted Merton, after practising a few minutes. "Funny that I never noticed that before. But none of the fellows in the Pacific Coast League noticed it, either. They didn't steal much on me there."

"That's just because they were minor leaguers," returned Joe. "But you're in big-league company now, and the wise birds on the other teams get on to you at once."

Merton was grateful for the tip, and practised assiduously until he had got rid of the mannerism. He was docile and willing to learn, and Joe could see his pitching ability increase from day to day.

Not only in pitching, but in batting, Joe was able to be of incalculable value to the younger members of the team. How to outguess the pitcher, when to wait him out, how to walk into the ball instead of drawing away from it, the best way of laying down bunts—these and a host of other things in which he was a past master were freely imparted to his charges and illustrated by object lessons that were even more effective than the spoken word.

McRae and Robbie were delighted with the results of the change of captains, and more and more they gave him a free hand, knowing that Joe would get out of the Giants all that was in them. And, knowing the power of the Giant machine when going at full speed, that was all that they asked.

The next series on the Giants' schedule was with the Boston Braves on the latter's grounds. As Joe had anticipated, the Braves put up a much stiffer fight than they had earlier in the season. They were going well, had already passed the Phillies and the Cardinals and were making a desperate attempt to get into the first division.

Markwith pitched the first game, and did very well until the last two frames. Then a veritable torrent of hits broke from the Bostons' bats and drove the southpaw from the mound. Joe took his place, and the hitting suddenly ceased. But the damage had already been done, and the game was placed in the Boston column.

Jim pitched in the second game and chalked up a victory. Young Merton was given his chance in the third, and justified Joe's confidence by also winning, although the score was close.

Joe himself went in for the fourth and won, thus getting three out of four in the series, which, for a team on the road, was not to be complained of.

With the Phillies, on the latter's grounds, the Giants cleaned up the first three games right off the reel. In the fourth, the Phillies woke up and played like champions. They fielded and batted like demons, so well indeed that when the ninth inning began, the Phillies were ahead by a score of three to two.

In the Giants' half, with one man on base, Joe cut loose with a homer that put his team a run to the good. Not daunted, however, the Phillies came in for their half.

Two men were out, and a couple of Giant fumbles had permitted two to get on the bases.

Mallinson, the heaviest batter of the Phillies, was up. He shook his bat menacingly and glared at Joe. With the team behind him the least bit shaky on account of the fumbles, Joe tried a new stunt on Mallinson.

"I'm going to tell you exactly the kind of a ball I'm going to throw to you," he remarked, with a disarming grin.

"Yes, you are," sneered Mallinson, unbelievingly, while even Mylert, the Giant catcher, looked bewildered.

"Honest Injun," declared Joe. "This first one is going to be a high fast one right over the plate and just below the shoulder."

"G'wan and stop your kidding," growled the burly Philadelphia batter.

He set himself for a curve, not believing for a moment that Joe would be crazy enough to tell him in advance what he was going to pitch. It was just on that disbelief that Joe had counted.

Joe wound up and hurled one over exactly as he had promised. Mallinson, all set for a curve, was so flustered that he struck at it hurriedly and missed.

Joe grinned tantalizingly, while Mallinson glowered at him.

"Didn't believe me, did you?" Joe asked. "Why don't you have more faith in your fellow men? I ought to be real peeved at you for your lack of confidence. But I'm of a forgiving nature and I'll overlook it this time."

"Cut it out," snapped Mallinson savagely. "Go ahead and play the game."

"No pleasing some fellows," mourned Joe plaintively. "Now this time, I'm going to pitch an outcurve. Ready? Let's go."

Mallinson, sure that this time he was going to be double-crossed, got ready for a high fast one, and the outcurve that Joe pitched cut the corner of the plate and settled in Mylert's glove for the second strike.

"You see!" complained Joe. "There you are again. What's the use of my tipping you off if you don't take advantage? Don't you believe me? Doesn't anybody ever tell the truth in Philadelphia?"

Mallinson tried to say something, but he was so mad that he could only stutter, while his face looked as though he were going to have a fit of apoplexy.

"Now," said Joe, "this is your last chance. I'm going to give you my hop ball this time, and that's just because it's you. I wouldn't do it for everybody. It'll take a jump just as it comes to the plate."

By this time Mallinson was in an almost pitiable state of bewilderment. Would the pitcher again keep his word? Or would Joe figure that now that he had twice tipped him off correctly, Mallinson would really get set for the hop ball and that now was the time to fool him with something else?

He was so up in the air by this time that he could not have hit a balloon, and he struck six inches below the hop ball that Joe sent whistling over the plate for an out. The game was over and the Giants had won.

"What was all that chatter that was going on between you and Mallinson?" asked McRae, as he and Robbie, with their faces all smiles, came up to Joe. "I couldn't quite get what it was from the bench. But you seemed to get his goat for fair."

Joe told them, and the pair went into paroxysms of laughter, Robbie choking until they had to pound him on the back.

"For the love of Pete, Mac!" he gurgled, as soon as he could speak, "you'll have to do something with this fellow or he'll be the death of me yet. To win a ball game just by telling the batsman what he was going to pitch to him! Did you ever hear anything like it before in your life?"

"I never did," replied the grinning McRae.

At the clubhouse later, there were guffaws of laughter as Mylert described the way that Joe had stood Mallinson on his head.

"And me thinking Joe had simply gone nutty!" Mylert said. "When he pitched that first ball just as he said, I didn't know where I was at. Then the second one got me going still more. But I saw that it had Mallinson going, too, and then I began to catch on. How on earth did you ever come to think of that, Joe?"

"Just a matter of psychology," Jim answered for him. "And mighty good psychology, if you ask me. Baseball Joe's a dabster at that."

"Sike-sike what?" asked Larry, whose vocabulary was not very extensive.

"Psychology," repeated Jim, with a grin. "No, it isn't a new kind of breakfast food. Joe simply knew how Mallinson's mind would work and he took advantage of it. Mallinson coppered everything Joe said to him. He figured that Joe was there to deceive him. He couldn't conceive that Joe would tell him the truth. And so it was just by telling the truth that Joe got him."

"It just got by because it was new," laughed Joe. "I couldn't do it often, for if I did they'd begin to take me at my word, and then they'd bat me all over the lot."

By the time the Eastern inter-city games were over, the Giants had considerably bettered their team standing. They had passed the Brooklyns, who had let down a good deal and were now playing in-and-out ball. The Chicagos were still in the lead, with Pittsburgh three games behind them, but pressing them closely. Then came the Giants, two games in the rear of the men from the Smoky City. The Cincinnati Reds brought up the rear of the first division, but the conviction was strong in the minds of the Giants that it was either the Pirates or the Cubs they had to beat in order to win the pennant.

On the eve of the invasion of the East by the Western teams, McRae called his men together for a heart-to-heart talk in the clubhouse.

"You boys know that I can give you the rough edge of my tongue when you lay down on me," he said, as he looked around on the group of earnest young athletes, who listened to him with respectful attention. "But you know, too, that I'm always ready to give a man credit when he deserves it. I'm glad to say that just now I'm proud of the men who wear the Giant uniform. You've done good work in cleaning up the Eastern teams. You've played ball right up to the end of the ninth inning, and many a game that looked lost you've pulled out of the fire.

"Now, that's all right as far as it goes. But the Western clubs are coming, and they're out for scalps. You remember what they did to us on our first trip out there. They gave us one of the most disgraceful beatings we've had for years. They took everything but our shirts, and they nearly got those. Are you going to let them do it again?"

There was a yell of dissent that warmed McRae's heart.

"That's the right spirit," he declared approvingly. "Now, go in and show the same spirit on the field that you're showing in the clubhouse. Beat them to a frazzle. Show them that you're yet the class of the League. Don't be satisfied with an even break. That won't get us anywhere. Take three out of four from every one of them. Make a clean sweep if you can. Keep on your toes every minute. You've got the pitching, you've got the fielding, you've got the batting, and you've got the best captain that ever wore baseball shoes. What more does any club want?"

"Nothing!" shouted Larry. "We'll wipe up the earth with them!"

"That's the stuff," replied McRae. "Now go out and say it with your bats. I want another championship this year, and I want it so bad that it hurts. You're the boys that can give it to me, and I'm counting on you to do it. Show them that you're Giants not only in name, but in fact. That's about all."

"What's the matter with McRae?" cried Curry, as the manager, having said his say, turned to leave.

"He's all right!" came in a thundering chorus from all except Iredell, who maintained a moody silence.

McRae waved his hand and vanished through the door.

The Cincinnati Reds were the first of the invaders to make their appearance at the Polo Grounds. They always drew large crowds, not only because they usually played good ball against the Giants, but especially because of the popularity of Hughson, their manager, who for many years had been a mainstay of the Giants and the idol of New York fans.

Hughson was one of the straight, clean, upstanding men who are a credit to the national game. McRae had taken him when he was a raw rookie and given him his chance with the Giants to show what he could do. The result had been a sensation. In less than a year Hughson had leaped into fame as the greatest pitcher in the country. He had everything—courage, speed, curves and control—and with them all a baseball head that enabled him to outguess the craftiest of his opponents.

For a dozen years he had been the chief reliance of the Giants and one of the greatest drawing cards in the game. At the time that Joe had joined the Giants, however, Hughson's arm was beginning to fail. The latter was quick to discover Joe's phenomenal ability and, instead of showing any mean jealousy, had done his best to develop it. Between him and Joe a friendship had sprung up that had never diminished.

Hughson's services were in demand as a manager and he was snapped up by the Cincinnati club to take charge of the Reds. With rather indifferent material to start with, he had built up a strong team that had several times given the Giants a hot race for the championship.

On the afternoon of the first game, Hughson, big and genial as ever, shook Joe's hand warmly when the latter met him near the plate.

"We're going to give you the same dose that we did when you were on our stamping ground the last time, Joe," he remarked, with a laugh, after they had interchanged greetings. "I love the Giants, but, oh, you Reds!"

"If you're so sure of it, why go through the trouble of playing the game?" retorted Joe.

"Oh, we'll have to do that as a matter of form and to give the crowd their money's worth," joked Hughson. "But honestly, Joe, we're going to put up the stiffest kind of a battle. My men have their fighting clothes on, and they're going good just now."

"I've noticed that," replied Joe. "You took the Pirates neatly into camp in that last series. The return of Haskins has plugged up a weak point in your outfield. I see he didn't lose his batting eye while he was a hold-out."

"No," said Hughson, "he's as good as ever. I began to think we'd never come to terms on the question of salary. You see, after his phenomenal season last year he got a swelled head and demanded a salary that was out of all reason. Said he wouldn't play this year unless he got it. But we got together on a compromise at last, and now he's in uniform again and cavorting around like a two-year-old. Wait until you see him knock the ball out of the lot this afternoon."

"I'll wait," retorted Joe with a grin, "and I'll bet I'll wait a good long while."

CHAPTER XIV

DEEPENING MYSTERY

After a little more chaffing, Joe left Hughson and walked over towards the Giants' dugout. He felt a touch on his shoulder and, turning around, saw Jackwell.

"What is it, Dan?" he asked, noting at the same time that the player was pale.

"I don't feel quite in shape, Captain," said Jackwell in a voice that was far from steady. "I was wondering whether you couldn't put someone in my place to-day."

"What's the matter?" asked Joe. "Look here, Jackwell," he went on sharply, "are you trying to pull some of that ptomaine poisoning stuff again? Because, if you are, I tell you right now, you're wasting your time."

"It—it isn't that," stammered Jackwell, nervously fingering his cap. "I just feel kind of unstrung, shaky-like. I'm afraid I can't play the bag as it ought to be played, that's all."

"Jackwell," commanded Joe sternly, "come right out like a man and tell me what's the matter with you. Lay your cards on the table. Are you playing for your release? Do you want to go to some other team?"

"No, no! Nothing like that!" ejaculated Jackwell, in alarm. "I'd rather play for the Giants than for any other team in the country."

"Well, I'll tell you straight that you won't be playing for the Giants or any other team very long if this sort of thing keeps on," said Joe sharply. "What do you think this is, a sanitarium for invalids? Here, McRae's taken you from the bush league and given you the chance of your lives with the best team in the country. Do you want to go back to the sticks?"

"Nothing like that," muttered Jackwell, twisting about uneasily.

"Then go out and play the game," commanded Joe. "I'm getting fed up with all this mystery stuff. There'll have to be a show-down before long, unless you get back your nerve."

Jackwell said no more and went back to the bench, where he had a whispered colloquy with Bowen, who seemed equally nervous.

When they went out to their positions, Joe noticed that both had their caps drawn down over their faces much more than usual. It could not have been to keep the sun out of their eyes, for clouds obscured the sky and rain threatened.

Fortunately, that is, for the Giants, for despite Hughson's prediction, it was not the Reds' winning day. Jim pitched for the Giants, and though he was nicked for seven hits, he was never in danger and held his opponents all the way. He did not have to extend himself, as his teammates, by free batting, gave him a commanding lead as early as the third inning, and after that the Giants simply breezed in.

Allison was the first of the Cincinnati pitchers to fall a victim to the fury of the Giants' bats. In the third inning, with the Giants one run to the good, Barrett, the first man up, sent a sharp single to left. Iredell followed with another in almost identically the same place, and an error by the Red shortstop filled the bases. Then Jackwell singled sharply over second, bringing in two runs.

It was clear that Allison's usefulness for that day was at an end, and Hughson replaced him by Elkins. Bowen lifted a sacrifice to Gerry in center and another run came over the plate. Mylert doubled and Jackwell scampered home. Curry hit to third and Mylert was tagged on the base line. Burkett was passed, as was also Wheeler. Then Joe, who, in the new shake-up of the batting order, occupied the position of "clean-up" man, justified the name by coming to the plate and hammering out a mighty triple that cleared the bases. There he was left, however, for Larry, up for the second time in the same inning, popped an easy fly that was gathered in by the second baseman. Seven runs had been the fruit of that avalanche of hits in that fateful inning.

From that time on it seemed only a question of how big would be the score. Two other pitchers were called into service by Hughson before the game was over, and although the torrent of Giant hits had almost spent its force, they came often enough to keep the Red outfielders on the jump.

In the eighth the Reds made a rally and succeeded in getting three men on bases with only one man out. But the rally ended suddenly when Jim made Haskins, the star batter of the Reds, hit to short for a snappy double play that ended the inning.

No further runs were made by either side, and the first game of the Western invasion went into the Giants' column by a score of ten to two.

In the clubhouse, after the game, Joe asked Jackwell and Bowen to stay after the others had gone, in order that he might have a word with them.

"I don't want to pry into your personal affairs, boys," he said to them kindly, when they were at last left alone. "I'd be the last one to do that. But I'm captain of this team, and I've got to see that my men are in fit condition to play. And if there's anything that prevents you showing your best form, it's up to me to find just what it is."

They made no answer, and Joe went on:

"I notice that whatever it is that's bothering you seems to affect you both. You both were sick, or said you were, at the same time the other day. You, Jackwell, told me that you were not feeling fit to-day, and although Bowen didn't say anything, I suppose it was because you told him it was of no use. I noticed that right after your talk with me, you went back to Bowen and held a whispered conversation with him. And when you went out on the field, you both pulled your caps over your faces more than usual.

"Then, too, neither of you played your usual game to-day. Luckily, we had such a big lead that the errors didn't lose the game, but in a close game any one of them might have been fatal. That was a ridiculously easy grounder, Jackwell, that you fumbled in the fourth, and in the sixth you failed to back up Iredell on that throw-in by Curry. And that was a bad muff you, Bowen, made of Haskins' fly to center, to say nothing of the wild throw you made to second right afterwards.

"Now, what's the trouble? Let's have a showdown. Speak up."

CHAPTER XV

TROUBLE BREWING

Still Jackwell and Bowen stood mute, neither of them venturing to meet Joe's gaze.

"If you don't tell it to me, you'll have to tell it to McRae," suggested Joe. "I'm trying to let you down easy, without calling it to his attention. If we can settle it among ourselves, so much the better. Is it some trouble at home that's weighing on your mind? Is it something about money matters? If it's that, perhaps I can help you out."

"That's very kind of you, Mr. Matson," said Jackwell, who seemed by common consent to be the spokesman for the two. "But it isn't either of those two. It's something else that neither Ben nor I are quite ready yet to talk about.

"I know very well that you have a right to know anything that's interfering with our playing the game as it ought to be played. And I'll admit, and I guess Ben will, too, that we were off our game to-day. But I think we'll soon be able to settle the trouble so it won't bother us any more.

"I wish you could see your way clear to give us a little more time. Let Ben and me have time to think and talk it over together. If we can settle the matter without letting any one else know about it, we'd much rather do so."

Joe pondered for a moment.

"I'm willing to go as far as this," he announced at last. "I'll give you a little more time, on this condition. If I note any further falling off in your play, or you come to me with any excuses to be let off from a game, I'm going to come down on you like a load of brick. Then you'll have to come across, and come across quick, or you'll be put off the team. Do you understand?"

"That's all right," said Jackwell. "You won't have any further cause to complain of me, Mr. Matson. I'll play my very best."

"I'll work my head off to win," declared Bowen.

They kept their promise in the series of games with the Western teams that followed. Jackwell played at third with a skill that brought back the memory of Jerry Denny, and Bowen covered his territory splendidly in the outfield. It seemed as though Joe's problem was solved, as far as they were concerned.

But the worry about them was replaced by another regarding Jim. There was no denying that the latter was not doing his best work. He was intensely loyal and wrapped up in the success of the team. But the opposing teams were getting to him much more freely than they had before that season. He was getting by in many of his games because the "breaks" happened to be with him, and because the Giants, with the new spirit that Joe had infused into them, were playing a phenomenal fielding game. But there was something missing.

There was nothing amiss in Jim's physical condition. His arm was in perfect shape and his control as good as ever. But his mind was not on the game, as it had formerly been. He worked mechanically, sometimes abstractedly. He was always trying, but it was as though he were applying whip and spur to his energies, instead of having them act joyously and spontaneously.

Joe knew perfectly well what was worrying his chum. Ever since that involuntary hesitation of Mabel's, when asked about Clara, Jim had been a different person. Where formerly he and Joe had laughed and jested together on the closest terms of friendship and mutual understanding, there was now a shadow between them, a very slight and nebulous shadow, but a shadow nevertheless. Jim's old jollity, the bubbling effervescence, the sheer joy in living, were conspicuous by their absence.

It was a matter that could not be talked about, and Joe, grieved to the heart, could only wait and hope that the matter would be cleared up happily. To his regret on his chum's account was added worry about the influence the trouble might have on the chances of the Giants.

For if there was any weak place in the Giants' armor, it was in the pitching staff. At the best, it was none too strong. Joe himself, of course, was a tower of strength, and Jim was one of the finest twirlers in either League. But Markwith, though still turning in a fair number of victories, was past his prime and unquestionably on the down grade. In another season or two, he would be ready for the minors. Bradley was coming along fairly well, and Merton, too, had all the signs of a comer, but they were still too unseasoned to be depended on.

If the deal for Hays had gone through, he would have been a most welcome addition to the ranks of the Giant boxmen. But the Yankees had had a change of heart, and had decided to retain him for a while.

So Joe's dismay at the thought of Jim, his main standby, letting down in his efficiency was amply justified.

The Cincinnatis came back, as Hughson had prophesied, and took the next game. But the two following ones went into the Giants' bat bag, and with three out of four they felt that they had got revenge for the trimming that had been handed to them on their last trip to Redland.

St. Louis came next, and this time the Giants made a clean sweep of the series. They were not so successful with the Pittsburghs, and had to be satisfied with an even break. But when the latter went over the bridge the Brooklyns rose in their might and took the whole four games right off the reel, thus enabling the Giants to pass them and take second place in the race.

Then came the Chicagos, who were still leading the League, but only by the narrow margin of one game. If the Giants could take three out of four from them, the Cubs would fall to second place.

Joe had made his pitching arrangements so that he himself would pitch the first and fourth games. He did so, and won them both. He had never pitched with more superb skill, strength and confidence, and the ordinarily savage Cubs were forced to be as meek as lapdogs.

They got even, to an extent, with Markwith, whom they fairly clawed to pieces in the second game. Jim pitched in the third, and but for a senseless play might have won.

That play was made by Iredell in the ninth inning, with the Giants making their last stand. The Cubs were three runs to the good. One man was out in the Giants' half, Curry was on third and Iredell was on second, with Joe at the bat.

Suddenly, moved by what impulse nobody knew, Iredell tried to steal third, forgetting for the moment that it was already occupied.

"Back!" yelled Joe in consternation. "Go back!"

With the shout, Iredell realized what he had done, and turned to go back. But it was too late. The Cub catcher had shot the ball down to second, and Holstein, with a chuckle, clapped the ball on Iredell as he slid into the bag.

A roar, partly of rage, partly of glee, rose from the spectators, and Iredell was unmercifully joshed as he made his way back to the bench.

Joe, a minute later, smashed out a terrific homer on which Curry and he both dented the plate. But the next man went out on strikes, and with him went the game. If Iredell had been on second, he also would have come home on Joe's circuit clout and the score would have been tied. The game would have gone into extra innings, with the Giants having at least an even chance of victory.

As it was, the Chicagos were still leading the League by one game when they packed their bats and turned their backs upon Manhattan.

McRae was white with rage, as he told Iredell after the game what he thought of him.

"You ought to have your brain examined," he whipped out at him. "That is, if you have enough brain to be seen without a microscope. To steal third when there was a man already on the bag! You ought to have a guard to see that the squirrels don't get you. What in the name of the Seven Jumping Juggernauts did you do it for?"

"I didn't know there was a man there," said Iredell lamely.

McRae looked as though he were going to have a fit.

"Didn't know a man was there!" he sputtered. "Didn't know a man was there! Didn't know a— Look here, you fellows," he shouted to the rest of the Giants gathered round. "I want you to understand there are no secrets on this team. You tell Iredell after this whenever there's a man on third. Understand?"

He stalked away from the clubhouse in high dudgeon to share his woes with the ever-faithful Robbie.

It was a hard game to lose, but Joe, as he summed up the results of the Western invasion felt pretty good over the record. The Giants had won eleven out of sixteen games from the strongest teams in the League, and were now only one game behind the leaders. They had climbed steadily ever since he had become captain.

But though he was elated at the showing of the team his heart was heavily burdened by his personal troubles. His mother was still in a precarious condition. He tore open eagerly every letter from home, only to have his hopes sink again when he learned that she was no better. Sometimes the strain seemed more than he could bear.

Then there was Jim, dear old Jim, with the cloud on his brow and look of suffering in his eyes that made Joe's heart ache whenever he looked at him. From being the soul of good fellowship, Jim had withdrawn within himself, a prey to consuming anxiety. He seemed ten years older than he had a year ago. And as a player, he had slipped undeniably. He was no longer the terror to opposing batsmen that he had been such a short time before. Joe gritted his teeth, and mentally scored Clara, who had brought his friend to such a pass.

But, troubled as he was, Joe summoned up his resolution and bent to his task. His work lay clearly before him. He was captain of the Giants. And the Giants must win the pennant!

CHAPTER XVI

OUT FOR REVENGE

"Joe," said McRae, on the eve of the Giants' second trip West, "I want to have a serious talk with you."

"That sounds ominous, Mac," replied Joe, with a twinkle in his eye. "What have I been doing?"

"What I wish every member of the team had been doing," responded McRae. "Pitching like a wizard, batting like a fiend, and playing the game generally as it's never been played before in my long experience as a manager. No, it isn't you, Joe, that I have to growl about. You're top-notch in every department of the game, and as a captain you've more than met my expectations. You've brought the team up from the second division to a point where any day they may step into the lead."

"Give credit to the boys," said Joe, modestly. "They're certainly playing championship ball. That is, with one exception," he added hesitatingly.

"With one exception," repeated McRae. "Exactly! And it's just about that exception I want to talk to you. Of course, we're both thinking of the same man—Iredell."

Joe nodded assent.

"I've worked myself half sick trying to brace him up," he said. "But he's taken a bitter dislike to me since he was displaced as captain of the team. He only responds in monosyllables, or oftener yet with a grunt. He's such a crack player when he wants to be that I've been hoping he'd wake up and change his tactics."

"Same here," said McRae. "He's been with the team for a long time, and for that reason I've been more patient with him than I otherwise would. But there comes a time when patience ceases to be a virtue, and I have a hunch that that time is now."

"You may be right," assented Joe. "I'm sorry for Iredell."

"So am I," replied McRae. "I'm sorry to see any man throw himself away. And that's just what Iredell is doing. If it were only a slump in his playing, such as any player has at times, it would be different. But it's more than that. I've had detectives keeping track of him for the last week or two, and they report that he has been drinking and frequenting low resorts. You know as well as I do, that no man can do that and play the game. So I'm going to bench him for a while and see if that doesn't bring him to his senses. If it does, well and good. If it doesn't, I'll trade him at the end of the season."

"That'll mean Renton in his place," said Joe, thoughtfully.

"Do you think he measures up to the position?" inquired McRae.

"I'm inclined to think he will," affirmed Joe. "Of course, he isn't the player that Iredell is when he's going right. But he'll certainly play the position as well as Iredell has since we returned from the last trip. He is an upstanding, ambitious young chap, and he'll play his head off to make good. He has all the earmarks of a coming star. With Larry on one side of him and Jackwell on the other, and with you and me to drill the fine points of the game into him, I think he'll fill the bill."

"Then it's a go," declared McRae. "I'll have a talk with Iredell to-night. You tell Renton that he's to play short to-morrow, and that it's up to him to prove that he's the right man for the job."

Joe did so, and the young fellow was delighted to learn that his chance had come.

"I'll do my best, Mr. Matson," he promised, "and give you and the team all I've got. If I fall down, it won't be for the lack of trying."

Pittsburgh was the first stop on the Giants' schedule, and Forbes Field was crowded to repletion when the teams came out on the field. The local fans had been worked up to a high pitch of enthusiasm by the closeness of the race, and they looked to see their favorites put the Giants to rout, as they had on the first visit of the latter to the Smoky City.

"Look who's here," said Jim to Joe, as the two friends drew near to the grandstand before the preliminary practice.

"Meaning whom?" asked Joe, as his eyes swept the stands without recognizing any one he knew.

"In the second row near that post on the right of the middle section," indicated Jim.

Joe glanced toward that part of the stand, and gave a violent start of surprise, not unmixed with a deeper emotion.

"That lob-eared scoundrel, Lemblow!" he ejaculated. "And confabbing with Hupft and McCarney."

"Evidently as thick as thieves," commented Jim. "A precious trio. I wonder they have the face to show themselves at a baseball game when they've done the best they could to bring the sport into disgrace."

"Three of the worst enemies we have in the world," murmured Joe, as his mind ran over the exciting events of the previous season.

Hupft and McCarney had been members of the Giant team that year. They were good players, but had entered into a conspiracy with a gang of gamblers—who had bet heavily against the Giants—to lose the pennant. Lemblow was a minor-league pitcher who had long wanted to get a chance to play with the Giants. If Joe, their star pitcher, could be put out of the game, Lemblow figured that his chance for a berth would be better. He also, therefore, had fallen in with the plans of the gambling ring, and had, seemingly, stopped at nothing to bring Joe to grief. How their plans miscarried, how Hupft and McCarney had been put on the blacklist that debarred them forever from playing in organized baseball, how Lemblow had been exposed and disgraced, are familiar to those who have read the preceding volume of this series.

"Wonder what they're doing here," puzzled Joe.

"Rogues naturally drift together," said Jim. "I heard some time ago that the bunch was playing with one of the semi-pro teams in the Pittsburgh district. But they usually play only on Saturdays and Sundays, so I suppose they're choosing this way to spend their off time. I suppose if we could hear what they're saying about us at this moment, our ears would be blistered."

"Whatever it is doesn't matter," laughed Joe. "They made acquaintance with our fists once, and I don't think they're anxious to repeat the experience. But I guess we'd better pick out catchers and begin to warm up. I've a hunch that the Pirates are going to pitch Miles to-day, and if they do we'll need the best we have in stock to turn them back."

By the time the bell rang for the beginning of the game, the stands were black with spectators. The Giant supporters were comparatively few, but they made up in vehemence what they lacked in numbers.

From the beginning it was evident that the game would be a pitchers' duel. Miles was in superb form, and up to the ninth inning had only given three hits, and these so scattered that no runs resulted.

But Joe was in the box for the Giants and was pitching for a no-hit game. Up to the ninth, not even the scratchiest kind of hit had been registered from his delivery.

Could he keep it up? The crowd waited breathlessly for the answer.

CHAPTER XVII

STEALING HOME

With Burkett, Barrett and Joe at the bat for the Giants in their half of the ninth inning, it looked as though the nine might have a chance to score.

But Miles had turned those same batters back earlier in the game, and he nerved himself to repeat.

"Murderer, are you?" he sneered, as the burly Burkett came to the bat, and referring to a nickname gained because of the many balls "killed." "Well, see me send you to the electric chair."

"Aw, pitch with your arm instead of your mouth," retorted Burkett. "You're due to blow up anyway. You're only a toy balloon, and I'm going to stick a pin in you."

But Miles had the last laugh, for he fanned Burkett with three successive strikes, and the latter went sheepishly back to the bench.

"That pin must have lost its point," Miles called after him. "I knew you were bluffing all the time."

Larry came up to the plate, swinging three bats. He threw away two of them and faced the pitcher.

"Why don't you throw that one away too?" queried Miles. "You might as well, for all the good it's going to do you."

"Your name is Miles, ain't it?" asked Larry. "Well, that's the way I'm going to hit the ball — miles."

He lunged savagely at the first ball that came over the plate and lashed it into the crowded grandstand for what would have been a sure homer, if it had not been a few inches on the wrong side of the foul line.

Larry kicked at the decision, but to no avail, and he came back disappointedly to the plate. But the mighty clout had sobered Miles somewhat, and the next two were out of Larry's reach and went as balls. Larry fouled off the next for strike two, and let the next go by for the third ball.

"Good eye, Larry," called Joe approvingly. "He's in the hole now and will have to put the next one over. Soak it on the seam."

Larry caught the next one fairly, and it started on a journey between right and center. Platz, the Pirate rightfielder, took one look at it and turned and ran in the direction the ball was going. At the back of the park was a low fence that separated the field from the bleachers. Just as the ball was passing over this, Platz reached out his hand and grabbed it. The force of the ball and the rate at which he was running carried him head over heels to the other side, but when he rose, the ball was in his hand.

It was a magnificent catch, and well deserved the thunderous applause that rose from the stand, applause in which even the Giant supporters joined, though it seemed to sound the death knell of their hopes.

"Hard luck, old man, to be robbed that way," said Joe consolingly, as Larry came back, sore and muttering to himself.

"To crack out two homers in one turn at bat and not even get a hit," mourned Larry. "Sure, if I was starvin' and it started to rain soup, I'd be out in it with only a fork to catch it with."

Joe received a generous hand as he came to the bat, due not only to his general popularity but to the wonderful game he had so far pitched.

"Oh, you home-run king!" shouted an enthusiastic fan. "Show them that you deserve the name. Win your own game."

"Watch Miles pass him," yelled another.

Whether Miles was deliberately trying to pass him, Joe could not tell. In any event, the first two balls pitched were wide of the plate, and the crowd began to jeer.

The third was by no means a good one, but still it was within reach, and Joe reached out and hit it between third and short to leftfield. With sharp fielding it would have gone for only a clean single, but the leftfielder fumbled it for a moment, and Joe, noting this, kept right on to second, which he reached a fraction of a second before the ball.

That extra base was worth a great deal at that stage, for now a single would probably bring Joe in for the first and perhaps the winning run of the game.

But would that single materialize? There were already two men out, and the chances were always against the batter.

Joe noticed that Miles was getting nervous. Wheeler was at the bat, and Miles was so anxious to strike him out that he was more deliberate than usual in winding up. Joe took a long lead off the bag, and watched the pitcher with the eye of a hawk.

The first ball whizzed over the plate for a strike. Joe noted that Wheeler hit full six inches under the ball. Evidently his batting eye was off. There was little to be hoped for from that quarter.

When Miles started his long wind-up, Joe darted like a flash for third. The startled catcher dropped the ball, and Joe came into the bag standing up.

"Easy to steal on you fellows," Joe joshed Miles, as he danced around the bag.

"That's as far as you'll get," snapped Miles. "I've got this fellow's number."

And Joe was inclined to think he was right, for when the next ball went over, Wheeler missed it "by a mile." One more strike, and the inning would be over.

Jamieson, the Pirate catcher, threw the ball back to Miles. Before it had fairly left his hand Joe was legging it to the plate. There was a yell from the spectators, and Miles, aghast at Joe's audacity, threw hurriedly to Jamieson.

Twenty feet from the plate, Joe launched himself into the air and slid into the rubber in a cloud of dust. The ball had come high to Jamieson, and he had to leap for it. He came down with it on Joe like a thunderbolt, and the two rolled over and over.

"Safe!" cried the umpire.

CHAPTER XVIII
A TEST OF NERVE

The play was so close and so much depended on it that there was a rush of Pirate players to the plate to dispute the decision. But the umpire refused to change it, and curtly ordered them to get back into the game.

Joe picked himself up, and, smiling happily, walked into the Giants' dugout, where he was mauled about by his hilarious clubmates, while McRae and Robbie beamed their delight.

"You timed that exactly, Joe," cried Robbie, "and you came down that base path like a streak. It's plays like that that stand the other fellows on their heads. Look at Miles. He's mad enough to bite nails. You've got his goat for fair."

"It looks like the winning run," said McRae. "And it's lucky that you didn't depend on Wheeler to bring you in, for there goes the third strike. Now it's up to you to hold the Pirates down in their last half."

"And rub it in by making it a no-hit game," adjured Robbie, as Joe put on his glove and went out to the box.

Joe needed no urging, for his blood was up and his imagination was fired by the prospect of doing what had not been done in either League so far that season.

But the Pirates were making their last stand in that inning, and he knew that he would have his work cut out for him. Their coachers were out on the diamond, trying to rattle him and waving their arms to get the fans to join in the chorus. From stands and bleachers rose a din that was almost overpowering.

Joe sized up Murphy, the first man up, and sent one over that fairly smoked. Murphy lashed out savagely and hit only the empty air.

"Strike one!" cried the umpire.

Murphy gritted his teeth, got a good toe hold, and prepared for the next. Joe drifted up a slow one that fooled him utterly.

Then for the third, Joe resorted to his fadeaway, and Murphy, baffled, went back to the bench.

Jamieson, who succeeded him, gauged the ball better and sent it on a line to the box. A roar went up that died away suddenly when Joe thrust out his gloved hand, knocked it down and sent it down to first like a bullet, getting it there six feet ahead of the runner.

Then Miles, the last hope, came up, and Joe wound up the game in a blaze of glory by letting him down on three successive strikes.

The Giants had won 1 to 0 in the best-played game of the year. The newspaper correspondents exhausted their stock of adjectives in describing it in the next day's papers.

Only twenty-seven men had faced Joe in that game. Not a man had reached first. Not a pass had been issued. Not a hit had been made. It was one of the rarest things in baseball—a perfect game.

And as the crowning feature, the one run that gave the victory to the Giants had been scored by Joe himself by those dazzling steals to third and home.

It was a good omen for the success of the Western trip, and the Giant players were jubilant.

"No jinx after us this time," chuckled Larry.

"If there is, he got a black-eye to-day," laughed Jim. "Gee, Joe, that was a wonderful game. You won it almost by your lonesome. The rest didn't have much to do."

"They had plenty," corrected Joe. "More than one of those Pirate clouts would have gone for a hit if it hadn't been for the stone-wall defense the boys put up. No man ever won a no-hit game with bad playing behind him."

At the hotel table that night Joe noticed that Iredell was not present.

"Wonder where Iredell is," he remarked to Jim, who was sitting beside him.

"Search me," answered the latter. "He may be in later. He's so grouchy just now that he seems to be keeping away from the rest of the fellows as much as he can. You can't get a pleasant word out of him these days. I spoke to him to-day on the bench, and he nearly snapped my head off."

"Too bad," remarked Joe, regretfully. "I've gone out of my way to be friendly with him, but he won't have it. Seems to think that I'm to blame for all his troubles."

They would have been still more concerned about the missing member of the team, could they have seen him at that moment.

Iredell, on his way to the hotel, had drifted into one of the low resorts which ostensibly sold only soft drinks, but where it was easy enough to get any kind of liquor in the back room. To his surprise, he saw Hupft, McCarney and Lemblow sitting at one of the tables.

There was a momentary hesitation on the part of the trio before they ventured to speak to him, for they did not feel sure how their advances would be received. But a glance at his face showed that he was in a dejected and reckless mood, and that decided them.

"Hello, Iredell," called out McCarney, with an assumption of boisterous cordiality. "Sit down here and take a load off your feet. Have something with us at my expense."

Three months before, Iredell would have scorned the invitation. Now he accepted it.

They talked of indifferent matters, the others studying Iredell intently.

"I noticed you weren't playing to-day," remarked McCarney, with a sickly grin.

"No," said Iredell, bitterly. "I ain't good enough for the Giants any more. They've benched me and put that young brat, Renton, in my place."

"Case of favoritism, I suppose," said McCarney, sympathetically. "Why, you can run rings around Renton when it comes to playing short!"

"That fellow, Matson, has got it in for me," growled Iredell. "But I'll get even with him yet."

"Sure, you will," broke in Hupft. "Nobody with the spirit of a man would take that thing lying down. He's jealous of you, that's what he is. You've been captain once, and he's afraid you may be again, and so he wants to freeze you off the team."

CHAPTER XIX

THE WARNING BUZZ

"Matson has a swelled head," declared McCarney. "He thinks he's the whole show. He's done us dirt, and now he's thrown you down. Are you going to stand for it?"

"No, I'm not!" snarled Iredell, now in the ugliest of moods. "I'll get even with him if it's the last thing I do."

"That's the way I like to hear a man talk," said Lemblow. "I owe him a lot for the way he's treated me, and so does every man here. We all hate him like poison. Then why don't we do something? It ought to be easy enough for the four of us to figure out some way to put the kibosh on him."

"It would be easy enough if he weren't so much in the limelight," said Hupft, uneasily. "If we put anything across on him, the whole country would be ringing with it. The League itself would spend any amount of money to run us down."

"Bigger men than he is have got theirs," rejoined McCarney. "It all depends on the way it's done. Now, a scheme has popped into my head while we've been talking. I don't know how good it is, but I think it may work. If it goes through, we'll have our revenge. If it doesn't we'll be no worse off and we can try something else. Now listen to me."

They put their heads together over the table, while McCarney in a low voice unfolded his scheme. That it was a black one was evident from the involuntary start the others gave when it was first broached. But as McCarney went on to explain the impunity with which he figured it could be carried out and the completeness of their revenge if it succeeded, they gave their adhesion to it. Iredell was the most reluctant of the four, but his drink-inflamed brain was not proof against the arguments of the others, and he finally acquiesced and put up his share of the estimated expense.

The next day witnessed another battle royal between the Giants and the Pirates. Jim pitched, and although his work was marked by some of the raggedness that Joe knew only too well the reason for, he held the Pittsburghs fairly well, and the Giants batted out a victory by a score of 7 to 3.

"Sure of an even break, anyway, on the series," remarked Curry complacently, after the game.

"Yes," replied Joe. "But that doesn't get us anywhere. That only shows that we're as good as the other fellows. We want to prove that we're better. To play for a draw is a confession of weakness. I want the next two games just as hard as I wanted the first two. That's the spirit that we've got to have, if we cop the flag."

But though Markwith twirled a good game the next day and was well supported, the best he could do was to carry the game into extra innings, and the Pirates won in the eleventh.

"Beaten, but not disgraced," was Joe's laconic comment, as he and Jim made their way to the hotel. "Let's hope we'll have better luck to-morrow."

"I've had a box sent up to your room, Mr. Matson," said the hotel clerk, as he handed the young captain his key. "It came in a little while ago."

"Thanks," said Joe, and went upstairs with Jim to the room they occupied together.

In the corner was a wooden box, about two feet long, a foot wide, and of about the same depth. On the top was Joe's name and the address neatly printed, but nothing else, except the tag of the express company.

"Wonder what it is," remarked Joe, with some curiosity.

"It isn't very heavy," said Jim, as he lifted it and set it down again. "Some flowers for you perhaps from an unknown admirer," he added, with a grin.

"It's nailed down pretty tightly," said Joe. "Got anything we can open it with?"

"Nothing here," answered Jim, as he searched about the room. "Guess we'll have to phone down to the office and have them send us up a chisel to pry the cover off."

"Oh, well, it will keep," said Joe. "I'm as hungry as a wolf, and I want to get my supper. We'll stop at the desk on our way back and get something from the clerk."

They had a hearty meal, over which they lingered long, discussing the game of the afternoon. Then they stopped at the desk, secured a chisel, and returned with it to their room.

Jim switched on the electric light, while Joe lifted the box and placed it on a table, preparatory to opening it.

"What's that?" Jim exclaimed suddenly, turning from the switch.

"What's what?" queried Joe in his turn.

"That buzzing sound."

"You must be dreaming," scoffed Joe. "I didn't hear anything."

"It seemed to come from the box when you lifted it up," said Jim. "Lift it up again."

Joe did so, and this time both of them heard a faint buzzing, whirring sound that, without their exactly knowing why, sent a little thrill through them.

Again he lifted it with the same result.

The two young men looked at each other with speculation in their eyes.

"Lay off it, Joe," warned Jim, as a thought struck him. "Perhaps it's an infernal machine."

"Nonsense," laughed Joe, though the laugh was a little forced. "Who'd send me anything like that?"

"There are plenty who might," affirmed Jim, earnestly. "Remember those crooks we saw at the game the other day! They hate you for exposing them. I wouldn't put anything past them. They'd go to all lengths to injure you."

Joe took out his flashlight and sent the intense beam all over the sides of the box. Suddenly he uttered an ejaculation, and pointed to a number of small holes, not visible on a casual inspection.

"Look!" he cried. "Air holes! Jim, there's some living thing in that box!"

CHAPTER XX

THE PACKAGE OF MYSTERY

"A living thing!" exclaimed Jim, in wonderment.

"Yes," replied Joe, whose quick mind had already reached a conclusion. "And I can make a guess at what it is. It's a rattlesnake!"

"What?" cried Jim, aghast. "Oh, no, Joe, you must be dreaming. No one would send you a thing like that."

"Well, I'll bet that somebody has," said Joe, grimly. "That would explain the buzz we heard just now. It was the whirr of the snake's rattles. We disturbed him when we lifted the box, and he's given us warning that he's on the job. Lucky we didn't open the box while it was on the floor. See here."

He lifted the box and let it fall with a sharp jolt on the table. This time there was no mistaking the angry rattle that issued from the box. They had heard it more than once when they had occasionally come across one of the deadly reptiles while out hunting. It was one of the sounds that once clearly heard could never be mistaken for anything else. Even now, with the box closed, it sent a thrill of horror through them.

Their faces were pale as they looked at each other and realized what might have been the fate of one or both of them but for that ominous warning.

"You see the dope?" questioned Joe, with an angry note in his voice. "I would be curious to see what had been sent to me, and would open the box probably with my face close above it. Then something would strike me like a bolt of lightning, and it would be good-night. I would have been out of the game with neatness and dispatch."

"The scoundrel!" ejaculated Jim, fiercely. "Oh, if I only had my hands on whoever did it!"

"I'd like to have a hand in settling that little matter, too," said Joe, with a blaze in his eyes that boded ill for the miscreant if he should ever be discovered. "But that can wait. The first thing to do is to put this rattler beyond the power of doing mischief."

Jim's eyes searched the room for some weapon.

"No," said Joe, "there's a safer way than that. That ugly head must never be thrust alive out of that box. Just turn on the water in the bathtub."

They had a private bath adjoining their room, and Jim turned on the tap. When the tub was half full, Joe brought in the box and put it in the tub, placing sufficient weight upon it to keep it beneath the surface of the water.

"Those air holes will do the business, I think," said Joe. "In a few minutes the box will be full of water. We'll leave it there a little while, and then we'll open the box and see if we guessed right."

At the expiration of twenty minutes, they drained the water out of the tub. Then Joe got the chisel, and with considerable effort forced open the cover of the box.

"You see," he said.

Jim saw and shuddered.

Lying in the water that was still seeping out through the air holes was a rattlesnake all of four feet long.

They viewed the creature with a feeling of loathing. But still deeper was the feeling they had against the scoundrels who had chosen that cowardly way of attempting to injure Joe. The snake, after all, was just the instrument. Infinitely worse were the rascals who had employed it as their weapon.

"We've had some pretty narrow escapes," said Joe. "And this is one of them. If you hadn't happened to hear that buzz, I might be a dead man this minute."

"It's too horrible for words!" exclaimed Jim, "It seems incredible that any one could plan such a thing for their worst enemy. Who do you think did it?"

"One guess is as good as another," replied Joe. "But if you ask me, I should say that the man or men who did it sat in the grandstand on the first day we played in this city."

"Lemblow, Hupft and McCarney," said Jim. "One or perhaps all of them. Well, why not? Lemblow tried deliberately to harm us both last year when he pushed that pile of lumber over from the scaffold above us. We came within an ace of being killed. If he were ready to harm us then, why shouldn't he be again, especially as he hates us worse now than he did before?"

"The box was certainly sent from somewhere in this city," said Joe, examining the cover carefully. "There's nothing to indicate that it came by railroad. And there are plenty of rattlesnakes in this part of Pennsylvania. Some of the stores exhibit them as curiosities."

"It's up to us to put the police on the trail right away," suggested Jim.

"I don't know about giving this thing publicity," mused Joe thoughtfully. "In the first place, it would create a sensation. It would be featured on the first page of every newspaper in the country. And you can see in a minute how it might react against baseball. The public would begin to figure that gamblers were trying to put the Giants out of the race. They haven't forgotten the Black Sox scandal that came near to ruining the game. We've got to think of the game first of all. You remember what hard work we had to save the League last year, and how we had to forego punishing the scoundrels in order to keep every inkling of the gamblers' scheme from the public. Baseball has to be above suspicion."

"Then do you mean to say that whoever did this is to get away scot free?" demanded Jim, hotly.

"No," said Joe, grimly, "I don't mean that. When the season closes, I'm going to make a quiet investigation of my own. And if I find the villains I'll thrash them within an inch of their lives and make them wish they had never been born. But they won't tell why I did it, and I certainly won't. At any cost, this thing must be kept from the public. The good of the game comes before everything else."

CHAPTER XXI

DROPPING BACK

"I suppose you are right, Joe," assented Jim, regretfully. "But it makes me boil not to be able to put the scoundrels behind prison bars. Those human snakes ought to have some punishment meted out to them."

"They surely ought," agreed Baseball Joe. "But we'll have to postpone their punishment. Everything will have to wait till the end of the season. Apart from anything else, if we found them out now and had them arrested, see how it would break into our work. We'd have to leave the team to come here to testify at the trial and perhaps stay away for weeks, and that would cost the Giants the pennant. But speaking of this fellow here in the box, what are we going to do with him? We can't leave him here."

"It's rather awkward," remarked Jim. "I suppose we could take him down to the cellar and have him burned in the furnace."

"Not without arousing the curiosity of the furnace man and leading to talk," objected Joe. "I'll tell you what we'll do. We leave town to-morrow night. We'll wrap the snake up in a compact package and carry it along in a suitcase. Then at night while the train is speeding along, we'll open a window and drop him out."

They agreed on this as the best solution.

"I suppose there's no question that the snake is dead," remarked Jim, with an inflection of uncertainty in his voice. "It would be mighty awkward to have him come to life again in the suitcase."

"I guess he's drowned all right," returned Joe. "He was a long time under water. But just to make assurance doubly sure, I'll cut off his head."

He took out his heavy jackknife and severed the reptile's head from his body. Handling the grisly creature was a repugnant task, and they were glad when it was finished.

"Guess I'll keep this head," remarked Joe, as a thought came to him. "I'll slip it into a jar of alcohol and that will preserve it indefinitely."

"What on earth do you want it for?" queried Jim. "I shouldn't think you'd care for that kind of souvenir."

"I have a hunch it may come in handy some time," answered Joe. "Now let's wrap up this body and get it out of our sight."

Their dreams that night were featured by wriggling, writhing forms.

"I'm glad I'm not scheduled to pitch to-day," remarked Jim, at breakfast. "I'm afraid the Pirates would bat me all over the lot. I never felt less fit."

"Such an experience isn't exactly the best kind of preparation for box work," replied Joe, with a ghost of a smile. "I guess Bradley will start, while I'll stand ready to relieve him if he gets in a jam. I'm hoping, though, that he'll pull through all right."

After lunch they took a taxicab to the grounds, but the vehicle got in a traffic jam, and it was later than they expected when they finally reached Forbes Field.

They hurried over to the clubhouse and were entering the door when they met Iredell, who was coming out.

Iredell gave a sharp ejaculation and started back, while his face went as white as chalk.

"Why, what's the matter, Iredell?" asked Joe.

"N—nothing," stammered Iredell, by a mighty effort regaining control of himself and walking away.

Their wondering glances followed him, and they noticed that his gait was wavering.

"What do you suppose was the reason for that?" asked Jim.

"I'm afraid he's been drinking again," conjectured Joe, regretfully. "His nerves seem to be all unstrung. When he looked at me, you might think that he saw a ghost."

"Perhaps he did," said Jim, slowly but significantly.

"What do you mean?" asked Joe, quickly.

"Just what I say," answered Jim. "Perhaps he thought that you were—well, in the doctor's hands, and that what he saw must be a ghost."

"You don't mean——"

"You know what I mean."

"No, no!" exclaimed Joe, in horror. "Lemblow, Hupft, McCarney? Yes! But Iredell! A man on our own team! A man we've played with for years! No, Jim, I can't believe it possible."

"Perhaps not," admitted Jim. "I hate even to think of it. I hope I'm wrong. But drink, you know, will weaken a man's moral fiber until he's capable of anything. Iredell's been steadily going to the dogs of late. Perhaps he's fallen in with McCarney's gang. He knows all of them, and a drinking man isn't particular about his company. Let a man hate you and then let him drink, and you have a mighty bad combination. Just suppose Iredell was in the plot. Suppose he knew that rattler was sent to you yesterday. Wouldn't he act just as he did when he saw you turn up safe and sound to-day?"

"It certainly was queer," admitted Joe, half-convinced. "I can only hope you're wrong. At any rate, it won't hurt to keep our eyes on him and be doubly on our guard."

Bradley showed more form that afternoon than he had before that season, and took the Pirates into camp in first class fashion by a score of 5 to 3. Apart from victory itself, it was gratifying to McRae and Robbie to note that Bradley was improving rapidly and furnishing a reinforcement to Joe and Jim, who, in a pitching sense, had been carrying the team on their backs.

Three out of four from so strong a team as the Pittsburghs was a good beginning for the swing around the Western circuit, and the Giants were in high feather when they arrived in Cincinnati.

"Hate to do it, old boy," declared the grinning McRae, as he shook hands with Hughson, "but we'll have to take the whole four from you this time."

"Threatened men live long, Mac," retorted Hughson. "Just for being so sassy about it, I don't think we'll give you one. Just remember the walloping we gave you the last time you were here. That wasn't a circumstance compared to what's coming to you now."

As it turned out, both were false prophets, for each team took two games.

"Five out of eight aren't so bad for a team away from home," Jim remarked.

"Better than a black eye," admitted Joe. "But still not good enough. We want twelve games out of the sixteen before we start back home."

It was an ambitious goal, but the Giants reached it, taking three out of four from the Chicagos and making a clean sweep in St. Louis. It was the best road record that the Giants had made for a long time past, and it was a jubilant crowd of athletes that swung on board the train for New York.

"I'm already spending my World Series money," crowed Larry, the irrepressible, to his comrades gathered about him in the smoker.

"Better go slow, Larry," laughed Joe. "There's many a slip between the cup and the lip. We haven't got the pennant clinched yet, by any means. And even if we win the pennant, there's the World Series, and that's something else again. It looks as though the Yankees would repeat in the American, and you know what tough customers they proved last time. And when Kid Rose gets going with that old wagon-tongue of his——"

"Kid Rose!" interrupted Larry, with infinite scorn. "Who gives a hoot for Kid Rose? What's Kid Rose compared with Baseball Joe?"

Joe's caution was justified by what followed after the Giants' return home. Suddenly, without warning, came one of the mysterious slumps that no baseball man can explain. If they had gone up like a rocket, they came down like the stick. They fielded raggedly, batted weakly, and fell off in all departments of the game. Perhaps it was the reaction after the strain of the Western trip. Whatever the cause, the slump was there.

McRae raged, Joe pleaded. They shook up the batting order, they benched some of the regulars temporarily, and put the reserve men in their places. Nothing seemed to avail. The "jinx" was on the job. The Phillies and Boston trampled them underfoot. In three weeks they had lost the lead, and the Chicagos and Pittsburghs had crowded in ahead of them.

Still Joe kept his nerve and struggled desperately to turn the tide. He himself had never pitched or batted better, and what occasional victories were turned in were chiefly due to him. But he was only one man—not nine—and the Giants kept on steadily losing.

Only one ray of light illumined the darkness for Baseball Joe. Mabel had come to him.

CHAPTER XXII

UNDER HEAVY STRAIN

"I can't believe you are real," said Joe, contentedly, lounging in a big chair and watching Mabel as she flitted about the room, putting small things in order and seeming by her very presence to make the hotel room a home. "I think you must be a dream or something. Come sit down here and let me look at you."

Mabel sat down beside him and looked at him with dancing eyes.

"I might almost think you were glad to see me, Joe dear," she said. Then, as Joe moved toward her, added quickly: "Do you know you haven't asked me a single thing about the home folks yet?"

Joe's face clouded and he rubbed a hand across his forehead.

"Truth is, I've been afraid to," he confessed. "I have a hunch that neither mother nor Clara has been frank in their letters to me. I've been worried sick!" he finished, in an unusual outburst of feeling.

Mabel, studying the new lines about his mouth and the strained look of his eyes, was inclined to be worried herself, though not so much for Mother Matson as for Joe. She said, as cheerfully as she could:

"I wouldn't worry so dreadfully, Joe, if I were you. Mother's heart is stronger than it has been for some time and she is wonderfully brave and courageous."

"She would be," muttered Joe, adding in swift anxiety: "In the last letter I had from her she said she was in the hospital and the operation was slated to take place in about a week's time. That would make it somewhere around day after to-morrow. Good heavens! I can't bear to think of it!"

"You mustn't, any more than you can help," said Mabel, gently. "It won't do Mother Matson or the rest of us any good for you to get down sick yourself, Joe. I wonder Dougherty doesn't order you off the team for a rest."

"You wrote in one of your letters that you had taken a flying trip to Riverside," Joe reminded her, and Mabel nodded.

"I didn't want to stay long. Mother Matson was so sick and I was afraid she would think she must exert herself to entertain me. So I just stayed overnight and caught the morning train back to Goldsboro."

"Did Mother give you any message for me?" Joe's voice was husky.

"Just her love—and this," said Mabel, softly. She held out her hand, and in the palm of it lay a tiny, heart-shaped locket. Joe recognized it as one that had long rested in his mother's jewelry case. He took it and opened it, and the sweet face of his mother in her youth smiled back at him.

Joe got up abruptly and went to the window, standing for a long time looking out, with his back to his wife. Mabel knew that he was having a struggle with himself, and waited quietly until he turned and came back to her.

"If I could get away from the team long enough to go to her!" he said huskily. "But I can't just now. It's impossible. I've got to keep after the men every minute, or they're apt to go to pieces."

"She doesn't expect you just now, dear," said Mabel, soothingly. "She knows you can't leave the team. Now don't worry."

Joe sank down in the chair again, his head in his hands. Finally he looked up and asked:

"How about Clara? Are things as bad there as we thought they were?"

"I'm afraid so, Joe. It seems to me that Clara is getting more and more entangled with that millionaire all the time. He reads poetry to her, too, in spite of the fact that he's a great, strapping, athletic looking chap."

"Oh, then you saw him?" cried Joe, all interest at once.

"Saw him!" repeated Mabel, with a short laugh. "You might better ask me if I saw anything else. He was around the place from morning to night. I think if Mother Matson hadn't been in such poor health he would have come around to breakfast, too."

Joe got to his feet and strode around the room, hands thrust deep in his pockets.

"Serious as all that!" Mabel heard him mutter to himself. "How does Clara act? How does she treat this—boob?" he demanded, suddenly stopping short in front of Mabel and glaring at her in exasperation. "Does she encourage him?"

"You might call it that," Mabel returned, with a puzzled frown. "She certainly accepts his attentions. Lets him take her out in his beautiful car, plays tennis with him, and listens while he reads his foolish poems to her."

Joe literally ground his teeth in futile rage and exasperation. He began again his restless pacing of the room.

"Did you have a chance to talk to her?" he continued his cross-examination. "Did you ask her what she meant by treating a fine fellow like Jim so shabbily?"

"You forget, Joe dear, that I'm not Clara's guardian. It wasn't my place to take her to task. All I could do was try to sound her. She evaded all my questions with some light answer, and when I asked her point-blank whether she intended to turn Jim down in favor of her millionaire — — "

"What did she say?" interrupted Joe, swiftly.

"She merely remarked that I ought to know better. She seemed to be offended, and if I had pressed things just then the result might have been a real quarrel. I thought the best thing to do was drop the whole thing. After all, Clara is old enough to know her own mind."

"I doubt it!" said Joe, bitterly, adding in helpless indignation as he again faced his wife: "Can you imagine any reasonably intelligent girl turning down good old Jim for a flossy millionaire?"

"Well, money sometimes dazzles a girl, especially young and very pretty ones like Clara," returned Mabel, judicially. "I tell you what let's do, Joe. I know it would be lovely to have our first dinner alone to-night, but don't you think we might include Jim? It might cheer him up."

"It would be an act of charity," agreed Joe. "Jim is pretty low in his mind these days. I'm sure he guesses there is something wrong."

But in spite of their whole-souled attempt to give Jim a good time that night, both Joe and Mabel felt that they had failed. Jim tried to rouse himself and meet their fun with some of his own, but nothing could disguise the fact that his heart was not in it.

He asked one or two listless questions about Clara, almost, Mabel thought, as though from a sense of duty, and after that maintained a dead silence on the subject they both knew was uppermost in his mind.

They had dined in a jolly restaurant full of lights and music, but despite the hilarity all about them, their party had been a dismal failure. They were glad when the last course was over and they could leave the place.

It was when they had reached the hotel and Mabel had slipped into another room to remove her hat and cloak that Joe turned to his chum with a casual question.

"Got your letter from Clara all right this week, did you?" he asked, in a tone that was not quite natural.

Jim looked at him, surprised, then turned away before he answered shortly:

"Not yet."

CHAPTER XXIII

BLUNDERING OLD REGGIE

"Oh, Joe, I do believe I'll go shopping to-day."

Mabel turned from the window where she had been standing looking down into the street. It was a glorious day, bright and sunshiny, and her face reflected the brightness of it.

"I do so like to shop in nice weather," she added, as she saw Joe's indulgent smile. "And if you like, I'll stop and buy you some gorgeous neckties."

"Dear girl, is that a threat or a promise?" teased Joe.

"Very well, I shall be completely selfish and buy everything for myself," Mabel promptly replied, adding with a sigh: "How you do wreck my generous impulses!"

"Didn't mean to, honey, honestly," said Joe, contritely, adding with a courage that none appreciated more than Mabel herself: "If you buy me a necktie, I swear to wear it whatever happens!"

Mabel made a face at him and disappeared into the other room, returning almost immediately with her hat and coat on.

"I won't have much time between practice and the game," Joe told her, as they went down together in the elevator. "So have a good time, girl. Take in a show if you like."

Mabel promised to enjoy herself, and a few moments later they parted in the sunny street, going their separate ways. Mabel turned to wave to him before she was swallowed up in the crowd, and Joe thought with a full heart how lucky he was.

"If I were in poor old Jim's place now, how would I feel?" he asked himself, and instinctively thrust the unpleasant thought away from him. He knew the agony of mind he would have suffered if at any time he had been in danger of losing Mabel, and pity for his chum took on a new intensity. He was almost afraid to meet Jim for fear of seeing that hopeless, lost look in his eyes.

"He certainly knows—or guesses—something," he told himself. "If I get a chance to-day I'll sound him out on the subject. After all, it sometimes helps a patient to have the wound lanced."

After the Giants had dropped another game, the chums, tired and disgruntled, turned their steps toward the hotel again. Jim seemed more than ordinarily depressed and met Joe's attempts at conversation with discouraging monosyllables. Several times Joe tried to lead up to the subject of Clara, only to be rebuffed by Jim's laconic replies.

After that Joe relapsed into silence, studying his chum thoughtfully. The thing was getting serious. Jim's silence and moroseness were growing on him. And the worst of it was that he did not seem to care. It was this very lethargy that Joe found most alarming. He would have welcomed an outburst of some sort, even condemnation of Clara and her actions. It was Jim's brooding taciturnity that baffled him.

They had almost reached the hotel when Joe felt a hand on his arm and turned to find himself confronted by a dazzling person. He blinked, and discovered that the vision was Reggie, dressed as always, in the latest fashion from smart soft hat to immaculate spats. Reggie swung his cane and beamed. Perhaps because the friendly face with its inevitable monocle was a welcome contrast to Jim's moodiness, Joe greeted his brother-in-law with more than usual enthusiasm.

"Say, but you're a sight for sore eyes, old chap!" he cried. "When did you blow in?"

"About an hour ago. Been busy all this time lookin' up a novel tie or two. Stopped in all the shops hereabouts and, bah Jove, the best they could show me was a creation of salmon pink with yellowish polka dots. No taste, no taste whatever, one might say!"

"Poor old Reggie!" said Joe, piloting him toward the hotel entrance and looking invitingly at Jim. "I'll put you wise to a couple of shops where you can get all the novel neckties you want. Come on upstairs, old boy, and see Mabel. She'll be pleasantly surprised. Coming, Jim?"

Jim hesitated for a moment, then nodded. The three stepped into the elevator and were swiftly shot up to the fourth floor. As they left the elevator, Reggie looked Jim over critically and gave vent to one of his too-frank observations.

"Lookin' rather seedy, old chap," he said. "Off the feed bag and sleepin' badly, eh?"

"Not at all. I'm feeling as fit as a fiddle," retorted Jim, brusquely.

The curt tone caused Reggie to look at the other in mild surprise, and, seeing that he was about to give voice to this emotion, Joe quickly changed the subject, keeping the conversation on safe ground until they reached the door of his rooms.

Mabel had not yet returned from her shopping expedition, and Joe felt curiously deserted as he led the way into the quiet place.

"Mabel is out buying up the department stores," he said. "Reckon she will be back most any time now. Tell us about yourself, Reggie. Every one well at home?"

Reggie glanced briefly at Jim, who had slumped into a chair and was staring abstractedly out of a window, then turned to Joe.

"Very well, old chap. In excellent health and spirits," he replied, puffing at a cigarette. "Missing Mabel, of course. It is really quite remarkable how that girl stirs things up. Bah Jove, it's a gift. Bally place gone dead without her, you know."

"Do you think you can tell me anything about that?" inquired Joe, with a humorously uplifted eyebrow. "I know all there is to know about missing Mabel!"

Jim turned from the window, rousing himself with difficulty from his abstracted mood.

"I think she's coming now," he said. "Thought I caught a glimpse of a red hat in the crowd. Guess I'll be going, Joe," he added, listlessly. "You three will have a lot to talk about."

"Hang around, old boy," urged Reggie, cordially, placing the monocle in his eye the better to stare at the disconsolate Jim. "Always regard you as one of the family, don't we? You would be offending Mabel by running away just as she arrives, you know. Stick around, old chap. She will be here presently. Ah, here she is now." He rose quickly, the monocle falling to his immaculate waistcoat, the most genuine pleasure on his thin face.

He took a step toward the door, but Joe was before him. He caught his young wife — and several bulky parcels — in a bear's hug, and when she emerged several seconds later, her face was flushed and the little red hat was set distractingly over one eye.

"Oh, Joe, and it was a new one, too!" she wailed, evidently referring to the hat. "I had such a gorgeous time. I bought and bought and bought— Who is that in the corner? Reggie, you old darling! Come here and give me a hug. Oh, this is just the best surprise ever."

"Rippin'. Had an idea you would like it all along," replied Reggie, complacently, as he favored his sister with a brotherly embrace. "You look perfectly stunning, you know. I say," he added thoughtfully, "did you see old Jim, hidin' over here in his corner? I take it your neglect is not intentional? No feud or the like, is there?"

"Oh, Reggie, don't be so silly," said Mabel, flushing a little as she went over to Jim. "I just didn't see him at first, that's all."

She held out her hand and Jim squeezed it heartily. There was a dumb suffering in his eyes that tugged at her heart. If she could only tell him something about Clara, something reassuring and heartening!

Mabel was in the midst of a laughing recital of her shopping tour when the telephone rang and Joe, answering it, found that McRae was in the hotel lobby waiting to speak to him. Reluctantly Joe excused himself, while Mabel disappeared into the other room to get ready for dinner.

Reggie, left alone with Jim, turned his quizzical gaze upon the latter. It was evident that Reggie was very much puzzled by Jim's strange behavior. And when Reggie scented a mystery he headed straight for the solution of it with a doggedness worthy of a better cause.

"Hard luck the team's been runnin' in lately, old chap?" he began.

"No hard luck about it. Bad playing. Bad team work," snapped Jim.

"Well, you shouldn't worry, anyway, old chap, you really shouldn't," reproved Reggie, mildly. "Bad for the game you know, and bad for the good old constitution."

Jim looked at him, a slow anger in his eyes.

"If I never had anything worse than my constitution to worry about, I'd be all right," he said, and turned his back upon Reggie, hoping that such action would terminate the conversation. But Reggie, in sublime ignorance, blundered on.

"I say, Jim, I've got it now. Worried because Clara couldn't come on with Mabel, eh? No doubt she wanted to come — rather. I say, old chap," he added, archly, lighting another gold-tipped cigarette, "better tend to your knittin'."

Jim, who had risen and was moodily pacing up and down, stopped and looked at Reggie.

"What's that?"

The quiet of his tone disarmed Reggie, who went on beaming pleasantly.

"Why, that millionaire who is hangin' around Clara, you know. Mabel has told you, hasn't she? Have I spilled the beans, Jim — let the jolly old cat out of the bag, and all that? Frightfully sorry. I thought you knew — —"

Reggie's explanations and excuses wavered into silence before the expression on Jim's face. At that moment he thought of nothing but escape, and with a few muttered phrases about "huntin' up Joe," blundered from the room, leaving Jim to his furious thoughts.

When, a few moments later, the door opened to admit Joe, Jim turned upon him, all the pent-up worry and nerve strain of the last few weeks finding vent in a flood of words.

"I knew you and Mabel were holding something back all the time, Joe. I've known from Clara's letters, for a long time, that something was wrong. If you're a friend of mine and have any regard for me, tell me about this millionaire who is hanging around Clara."

"Has Reggie — —"

"Yes, Reggie has!" retorted Jim, grimly. "Go ahead, Joe, and tell me the truth."

Seeing that there was nothing for it, Joe told all he knew about Jim's rival, glossing over the details and making as light of the whole thing as possible.

"So that's that!" said Jim, quietly, when Joe's explanation had stumbled into silence. "The end of everything!"

Joe, feeling deeply for his chum but powerless to comfort him, said, with a forced cheerfulness, "All this probably sounds a hundred times worse than it really is, Jim. When you go down there — —"

"If she wants to marry for money, let her!" interrupted Jim, with sudden ferocity. "Do you suppose I'd deprive her of her pet millionaire? Not much!"

CHAPTER XXIV

GETTING A CONFESSION

"It cuts me to the heart, Jim," said Joe, with deep feeling, laying his hand affectionately on his chum's arm. "I can't tell you how sick I feel about the whole thing. Nothing that affects you can fail to affect me. You know that, don't you, Jim?"

"Of course I do, Joe. You've been a brother to me ever since I joined the Giants. Whatever success I've had in my work has been due to your kindness, your teaching, your encouragement. Don't think I'll ever forget it. I shouldn't have burst out the way I did, but you can't know the misery I've endured in the last few weeks. It was bad enough when I only had a vague suspicion that things weren't right. Now it seems more than I can stand. It's hard, Joe, to see your house of cards come tumbling to the ground."

"I know it is, Jim," replied Joe, with warm sympathy. "But take it from me, Jim, your house hasn't fallen yet. I'm sure that Clara is true blue at heart, and that no matter how things look, there must be some explanation that will clear up everything."

"I hope so," said Jim, though there was not much hopefulness in his tone. "I've got to know soon or I'll go crazy. You see how this thing has knocked me out of my stride. I'm not pitching up to my usual form, and you know it."

"I've noticed it, of course," said Joe. "And I've guessed the reason. You've got all the old stuff, all the strength and cunning, but you haven't been able to use it because of the burden on your mind. Even at that, though, you've been turning in more victories than the other fellows."

"Which isn't saying much, the way the team is running now."

"All the more reason for taking a big brace, old boy!" exclaimed Joe, giving him a hearty slap on the shoulder. "Try to throw off your troubles and work your head off for the success of the team."

"I'll do it," promised Jim, as he shook his chum's hand to bind the bargain.

"Good," said Joe, heartily. "And promise me one thing, Jim. Don't hint at anything of this in your letters to Clara. Nothing can really be explained in a letter. Nothing in the world has caused so much estrangement, so much heartache, as trying to arrange a misunderstanding by letter. You can't say just what you want, and what you do say is never understood just in the way you want it to be. Wait until you can see Clara face to face, and I'll bet the whole thing will be cleared up in five minutes."

"But that will be at the end of the season!" exclaimed Jim, in dismay.

"Not so long as that, I guess," said Joe. "I'm going to see if I can't by some means get Clara to make a flying visit to New York." He paused a moment, and his brow clouded with anxiety. Then he resumed: "Of course she can't do it right now because my mother is in too critical a condition. But if the operation turns out all right and she has a good recovery, it might be managed. If not, I have something else in mind that I'll talk to you about later."

To Joe's already overburdened mind was added another worry in the game with the Bostons the next afternoon.

Jackwell and Bowen, while they had been affected by the general slump of the team, had given no evidence of a return of the peculiar nervousness that had marked their actions earlier in the season. But Joe noticed on that afternoon, the frequent looks at the stand and the pulling of their caps over their faces for which he had before taken them to task.

Merton was pitching, and Joe was playing in left. In the fourth inning, an easy fly came out to Bowen and he made a miserable muff. Jackwell also made a couple of errors at third. In each case the blunders were costly, as they let in runs.

"What made you drop that fly, Bowen?" Joe asked, as the Giants came in from the field.

"I lost it in the sun," replied Bowen. "At this time in the year the sun comes over the grandstand in such a way that it's right in my eyes."

"Haven't heard you complain of it before," remarked Joe, dryly. "For the rest of this game I'll play center, and you shift over to left."

The change was made accordingly. In the eighth inning another fly came to Bowen and again he dropped it while the crowd booed. The error let in what proved to be the winning run for the Bostons.

"I want to see you fellows after the game," said Joe, curtly, to the two men. "Wait around the clubhouse after the others have gone."

When the clubhouse was finally deserted by all but the three, Joe turned to them sternly.

"I'm fed up with this mystery stuff," he said. "It's got to end right here. It lost the game for us this afternoon, but it isn't going to lose another. Come across now and make a clean breast of it."

The two men looked at each other uncertainly.

"You heard me," said Joe. "Out with it now, or I'll see that you're fired off the team."

"All right, Mr. Matson," Jackwell spoke up with sudden resolution. "I'll tell you just what the trouble is. Ben and I are afraid that detectives are after us."

"Detectives!" ejaculated Joe, with a start. "What are they after you for? What have you been doing?"

"Nothing wrong," declared Jackwell, earnestly, and Bowen echoed him.

"Why should they be after you, then?" asked Joe, with a faint tinge of skepticism in his tone.

"We got mixed up in a shady business," explained Jackwell, with a look of misery on his face. "But we didn't know there was anything wrong about it till it went up with a bang. You see, Mr. Matson, this is the way it came about. Last winter, Ben and I were rather up against it—short of ready money. You know what poor salaries they pay in the league we came from. We were down in Dallas, Texas, and the oil boom was on. We saw an ad for men to sell oil stocks, and we answered it. The fellow at the head of it—Bromley was his name—was a smooth sort of chap and could talk any one into anything. From his description, we thought his oil well was an honest-to-goodness well, and we sold a lot of stock for him. Then came the blow-up, and it turned out that his well was just a dry hole in the ground. He got out from under just before the crash came, and I heard he went to Mexico. The federal officers got after him and all connected with it. We heard that warrants were out for us, and we skipped North. But until the company broke we thought they were straight as a string. We wouldn't have had anything to do with it if we had thought it was crooked. We were just roped into it. That's as true as that we're sitting here this moment. All that either of us got out of it was part of our salaries and part of the commissions that were promised."

CHAPTER XXV

IN THE DEPTHS

The story had a ring of sincerity that was not without its appeal to Joe. Still, he knew that some of the most plausible stories are told by the worst of crooks, and before accepting it fully he determined to make some investigations on his own account.

"Dallas is a long way from here," he remarked, as he eyed the two men keenly. "What makes you think the federal agents are looking for you?"

"Because we know some of the men that are in the Dallas branch," replied Jackwell, "and on several occasions we've seen one or more of them at the Polo Grounds and at other fields on the circuit."

"That doesn't say they're looking for you," said Joe. "I suppose all of them take in a game when they get a chance. Besides," he went on, as another thought struck him, "if they really wanted you, it would be no trick to get you. Your names appear in the papers in the scores of the game every day. Every one that follows the game knows Jackwell and Bowen."

"True enough," admitted Jackwell, a little shamefacedly. "But, as a matter of fact, we didn't go by our own names while in Dallas. You see we thought the rest of the baseball players would think that we were kind of hard up to be working in the season when most of them are resting. I can see now that it was a foolish sort of feeling. But, as Ben said, actors and actresses don't go by their right names, and authors use names that are not their own, and we had as much right to do it as they had."

"I suppose you had," admitted Joe. "Though in business I think it's a mistake not to go under your own name. What names did you go by?"

"Dan was Miller and I was Thompson," put in Bowen, who up to now had let Jackwell do most of the talking. "So you see they don't know Jackwell and Bowen, but they might recognize our faces, just the same. I suppose they have descriptions of us, and that's the reason we hate to go on the field when we see they're around."

"And why you pull your caps down over your faces when you do go out," added Joe. "Well, boys, I'm glad you've told me what's been bothering you. Perhaps the very telling will take some of the load off your mind. For the present, I'm going to take your word for it that you didn't knowingly do any wrong. But I tell you frankly that I'm going to have the matter looked up, and if you haven't told me the truth, you'll have to get off the team. McRae won't have any one on the Giants that isn't as white as a hound's tooth, as far as character is concerned.

"But in the meantime, you've got to play ball. We can't let your personal troubles interfere with the success of the Giants. There's been many a time when I've had a load of trouble on my mind, but I've played ball just the same. The chances are that you're magnifying this thing, anyway. You don't really know that there are any warrants out for you at all. You say you heard there were, but the chances are that if there were they'd have nabbed you before you heard anything about the warrants. Those government fellows don't hire a brass band to let you know they're coming. Perhaps you're tormenting yourselves about something that never happened. And even if it did, the agents have lots of bigger cases to look after, and they may have forgotten that you're alive. But whether they have or not, the thing that interests me just now as captain of the Giants, is whether or not you fellows are going to play the game. How about it?"

"I will, Mr. Matson," said Jackwell, with decision. "I'm going to put this thing out of my mind and play the game for all it's worth."

"Count me in on that," declared Bowen, with emphasis.

"That's the stuff!" returned Joe. "Just remember that the coward dies a thousand deaths while the brave man dies only once. Half the troubles that worry us in life are those that never happen. Now forget everything but that you're ball-players, that as honest men you owe your best services to the team, and that the Giants have got to win the flag this year. That's all for now."

The results of this heart-to-heart talk were not long in coming. Both Jackwell and Bowen seemed to brace up wonderfully. The former took in everything that came his way and made plays that seemed almost impossible. Bowen ranged the outer garden in first-class style and put Wheeler and Curry on their mettle to keep up with him.

The brace that they had taken was not long in communicating itself to other members of the team, and the Giants began to come out of their slump. A stern chase is proverbially a long chase, and it proved so in this case, for the Pirates and the Chicagos had made hay while the sun shone, and had piled up a commanding lead. But the case, though hard, was not yet desperate, and the Giants had not relinquished hope of coming out ultimately at the head of the heap.

As Joe had promised himself, he looked up the Dallas matter. He had fully made up his mind that if the men had been guilty of crookedness they would have to get off the team. He would miss their playing sorely, and would have all kinds of trouble in plugging up the holes that would be left by their departure, but anything was better than a scandal that would damage the game. Of course, the ultimate decision would be made by McRae, but Joe knew his manager well enough to feel sure that he would be in accord with him in this matter.

Joe got in touch with a lawyer, who in turn communicated confidentially with a Dallas law firm, asking it to make inquiries in the oil-well case and find out whether there had been any warrants or indictments out for men named Miller and

Thompson, and if so, to find out the exact charges on which the instruments were based.

A week or so elapsed before a reply was received. Joe tore the letter open eagerly and ran his eyes over the contents. Then he gave a shout of exultation and brought his hand down on his knee with a resounding slap.

"What's the matter?" asked Jim, looking up in some surprise. "Any one left you a million dollars?"

"Not exactly that," laughed Joe. "But I've just learned something that makes me feel mighty good, just the same."

His elation was caused by these words in the letter:

"In re Miller and Thompson, we beg to report that there were no warrants or indictments handed down for these men in the Bromley case. Investigation convinced officials that they had no guilty knowledge of the fraud. The only documents connected with them were subpœnas calling them as witnesses before the Grand Jury. Their testimony was not needed, however, as a true bill was found against Bromley, who is an international swindler with many aliases. He is believed to have fled to Mexico. A reward of five thousand dollars is offered for his capture."

"Maybe this won't be good news for Jackwell and Bowen," chuckled Joe, as he folded up the letter.

CHAPTER XXVI

OFF HIS STRIDE

Joe pitched the next day against the Phillies, and won a hard fought battle. Atkins, the Philly pitcher, was in capital form, and the game was a seesaw affair, first one and then the other getting the lead, and it was not until the ninth inning that the contest was decided.

Farley, the third baseman of the Quaker team, was a "rough house" player, who never hesitated to transgress the rules of the game, provided that he could get away with it.

One of his favorite tricks was to grab the belt of an opposing player as he rounded third base. This was often sufficient to throw the runner off his stride and slow him up for a second, and in a game where fractions of a second often marked the difference between a run and an out, the momentary delay many times permitted the ball to get to the plate before the runner.

He resorted to the same trick also, when the third base was occupied by an opponent and a long fly was hit to the outfield. If the ball was caught, the runner, of course, had to touch the bag after the catch before he started for the plate. Just as he started, Farley would grab his belt. The umpire's eyes would be on the ball to see if it were caught, and Farley could do this with impunity.

It was of little use complaining to the umpire, for that functionary, not having seen the action, could not well punish it. His eyes were his only guide in making decisions.

Twice in this series with the Phillies the Giants had lost in this way what would have been sure runs.

On the day in question, Joe had made a two-bagger and had got to third on a fielder's choice. There was but one man out, and the proper play at this juncture was a long sacrifice fly to the outfield.

Wheeler got the signal and obeyed orders. He sent out a towering fly that settled into the rightfielder's hands. The ball had gone high rather than far, which gave the outfielder a good chance to get it home in time to nail the runner.

If Joe was to make the plate, he had to get a quick start and do some fast running. The fly was caught, and Joe broke from the bag just as Farley grabbed his belt. But not for a second did Joe slacken speed. He flew along the base path at a rattling clip and beat the ball to the rubber by an eyelash.

With the roar that went up from the crowd was mingled boisterous laughter.

Farley was standing at third with a ludicrous look of bewilderment on his face, holding in his hand Joe's belt. He did not seem to know what to do with it, and shifted it from one hand to another as though it were a hot potato.

Joe had unfastened it on the sly as he stood at the bag, and when Farley grabbed it, it came away in his hand without Joe even feeling it. Farley had braced himself for the pull, and the lack of resistance nearly threw him to the ground. He had to stagger some steps before he could regain his balance.

Peal after peal of uproarious laughter at Farley's foolish appearance rose from the spectators. If ever there was a case of being "caught with the goods," Farley furnished it at that moment.

And the merriment swelled up anew when Joe walked out to third, and with his hand on his heart and a ceremonious bow, politely asked Mr. Farley to return his property. With his face flaming red from mortification, Farley threw it to him with a scowl and a grunt, and Joe with a tantalizing grin took his time in putting it on.

"Joe," said McRae, as he shook his hand, "when it comes to outguessing the other fellow there's nobody in the game that can compare with you. You spring things that nobody ever thought of before. To-day's an instance. More power to you, my boy."

Though the Giants had made an immense improvement over their previous recent showing, they were still far from the form they had showed on their last Western trip. And a great part of this, Joe had to admit to himself, was due to Jim's indifferent showing.

It was not that Jim did not try. He was intensely loyal to the team, of which he had been one of the principal supports. But the old spontaneity was lacking. He had to force himself to his work, where formerly it had been a joy to him. And no man can do his best work under those conditions. Twice within the last few weeks he had been batted out of the box.

"Joe," said McRae to his captain, "on the dead level, what is the matter with Jim? He isn't the pitcher he was last season or in the early part of this. What ails him?"

"I'll tell you, Mac," replied Joe, who saw the opening he desired. "Jim has heart trouble."

"What?" cried McRae, in consternation. "Did a doctor tell him so?"

"It isn't a case for a doctor," explained Joe. "The only one who can cure Jim's trouble is a certain girl."

"Oh, that's it!" exclaimed McRae with relief. "The girls! The girls! The mischief they make!"

"Don't forget you were young once yourself, Mac," said Joe, with a grin. "Now I want to ask you a favor. I have an idea that five minutes' talk with that girl will set things all right. Why not give Jim a few days off? I don't ask this simply because Jim is my friend. I think it will be for the good of the team."

"We're pretty hard up for pitchers," said McRae, dubiously.

"I'll double up while he's gone," promised Joe. "I'll pitch his game as well as my own. I'm as fit as a fiddle."

"You're always that," answered McRae. "Well, have it your own way," and he walked away muttering again: "The girls! The girls!"

"Jim," said Joe, later that afternoon, "how about taking a train to-morrow afternoon for Riverside?"

Jim jumped about a foot.

"Do you mean it?" he cried.

"Sure thing," replied Joe. "I've fixed it up with Mac."

"Glory hallelujah!" shouted Jim. "Joe, you're the best ever! Where's that suitcase of mine?"

CHAPTER XXVII

TAKEN BY SURPRISE

"At last I'll know where I stand, anyway," muttered Jim to himself, as the train sped on toward Riverside. "It wouldn't have done a bit of good to write to her. Her letters are so vague and unsatisfactory these days. I must see her. Then I'll be able to tell whether there is anything to this story of my millionaire rival."

He tried to make himself think that there was nothing in what Reggie had let slip, in what Joe had reluctantly told him. Surely, they had been mistaken. Clara, after all that had passed between them, could not treat him so shabbily!

And yet — the thought made him frown and bite his lip fiercely — where there was so much smoke it seemed certain there must be some fire. Long before he had known definitely of a rival with millions who had been besieging Clara with his attentions, he had thought he sensed a change in her attitude toward him. Her letters had not been so regular. Once or twice he had missed them altogether. Those that did come had left him vaguely disappointed, unhappy. The reason for his dissatisfaction had eluded him. Then suddenly, it had all become clear. Clara was being won away from him by a chap with more money than he had! He clenched his hands and his mouth became grim. At any rate he would have one satisfaction. He would tell this fellow just what he thought of him, and that in no uncertain terms! Perhaps the chap would give him some excuse for thrashing him. His eyes glinted and his fists clenched.

The swift motion of the train was grateful to him. It seemed to keep time with his hurried thoughts. But the knowledge that every mile of ground they covered brought him nearer to Clara was more terrifying than anything else. He thought of the last time he had boarded a train to go to his sweetheart, and the lines about his mouth grew deeper. He dreaded what he might find at the end of the journey.

He had expected a letter from Clara that morning, had hoped he would get it before leaving. But, as had been the case more and more often in the last few weeks, he had been disappointed, had been forced to start on his trip with no word from her.

He took out a magazine and tried to read. The words were a meaningless blur before his eyes, and he threw the magazine away from him with an exclamation of disgust. What good was he, anyway? He could not, even for a few moments, force his mind away from his troubles.

And so it was with a mixture of perturbation and relief that he at last came to an alert consciousness of his surroundings, to find himself at the next station to Riverside. He pulled himself together and prepared to face facts. His uncertainty was nearly at an end. It seemed to him that nothing that could happen in the future could be any worse than what he had already been through.

Before the train had stopped at Riverside, Jim had flung himself and his one bag on to the platform. He glanced about him quickly to assure himself that no old acquaintances were around the place, then started off at a brisk pace in the direction of the Matson home.

As he approached nearer his destination, he unconsciously slackened his pace. He had sent Clara no word of his coming. That part had been intentional. Since he was about to find out the truth, it would be far better to take the girl by surprise than to warn her of his coming and so give her time to prepare for it.

Perhaps, he thought bitterly, and his steps lagged still more, Clara would not even care to deceive him with a show of affection. This hatedmillionaire might even have dazzled her to the extent of a broken engagement with him, Jim.

At the thought, new anger kindled in him, and he strode forward with resolution. At the moment, all he cared about was a meeting with his rival. He did not know how soon that desire was to be gratified.

A turn in the road brought him within view of the pleasant Matson home. At the familiar sight of it, something swelled in Jim's throat. He had felt so a part of that household, had been so wonderfully sure of Clara's love. Could it be possible that all his faith had been misplaced, all his hopes and dreams only idle and vain imaginings?

The house was coming nearer, seemed to be rushing to meet him. With every step he dreaded more to know the secret it was hiding from him.

He had reached the gate, had swung it open noiselessly. The porch steps invited — the steps where he and Clara had often sat in the twilight, dreamily planning their life together. But for some reason he avoided them.

He had no desire to see any one but Clara just then, and instinct told him he would find her in the garden. So to the garden he turned, hungrily drinking in the fragrance of the flowers, the ache at his heart more poignant as each new and familiar object met his eye.

He heard voices and stopped still. One of them was Clara's. She was laughing lightly at some pleasantry directed to her in a deep, masculine voice.

At the sound, Jim suddenly saw red. All the anxiety, the worry, the heartache of the last few weeks, took toll at once. With a grumble of wrath away down in his throat, he almost ran the remaining few feet that hid from him the two in the garden.

Clara was sitting on a rustic bench. She wore a pretty dress of rosy material that matched the color in her cheeks. She was looking up at a blond giant whose attitude expressed complete devotion. The giant was speaking in the deep, musical voice which had so infuriated Jim.

"Miss Matson, I'm going to Europe in a few days and I must know if I have any chance at all with you. It isn't possible for me to go on this way — —"

"Good afternoon," said Jim, in a voice of suppressed emotion. "Sorry to intrude."

CHAPTER XXVIII

A FRESH SPURT

Joe had taken the first occasion to see Jackwell and Bowen alone after he had received the letter from Dallas.

"I've learned that there were papers out against you in Dallas in connection with that oil swindle," he said, with an assumed expression of gloom.

"Then they were after us, just as we thought!" exclaimed Jackwell, in alarm, while Bowen turned pale.

"They were after you all right, but only as witnesses," laughed Joe, tossing them the letter. "Read that."

The expression of relief and happiness that came to both, as they scanned the welcome lines, was good to see.

"I'd rather have that than a million dollars!" cried Jackwell, his face fairly beaming with delight.

"We can't thank you enough for such good news," said Bowen, equally jubilant.

"That's all right," said Joe. "I had a hunch right along that you fellows were on the square. All the thanks I want now is to have you play the game. You've been doing well lately, and I want you to keep it up."

"That isn't a circumstance to what we're going to do," promised Jackwell, and Bowen nodded assent. "From this time on, just watch our smoke."

And Joe had no reason to complain of their work for the rest of the season. With the incubus removed that had been lying on their spirits, they played like wild men, and their work soon enthroned them as favorites with the Giant fans.

Now the Giants were really climbing again, and the grounds began to be crowded as in the days of old. The games were played "for blood" from the ring of the gong.

And what put the capsheaf on Joe's satisfaction was that Jim came bursting in upon him one morning like a whirlwind, his face radiant, and sheer delight in living shining in his eyes.

Joe sprang up to greet him, and Jim grabbed him and whirled him around the room until both of them were gasping for breath.

"For the love of Pete, Jim!" expostulated Joe, laughingly.

"I'm a curly wolf!" shouted Jim. "I eat catamounts for breakfast and pick my teeth with pine trees! Where are those Cubs and Pirates and all the rest of that riffraff? Lead me to them! I want ber-lud!"

"You'll get your chance," answered Joe, grinning. "Now sit down and try to be sensible for a minute."

"Sensible!" scoffed Jim. "Who wants to be sensible? I'm happy!"

"And so am I," laughed Joe, "because of the news you bring."

"I haven't told you any yet," countered Jim.

"Yes, you have," declared Joe. "You've told me everything. I know that everything's all right between you and Clara."

"Clara!" repeated Jim, dwelling on the name. "Clara! Say, Joe, that sister of yours is—is— Oh, well, what's the use? There isn't any word in the English language to describe her. She's—she's——"

"Yes, I know," laughed Joe. "I'm her brother. Now, old boy, take a minute to get your breath, and then tell me the whole story."

So Jim perforce had to restrain his ecstasies and get down to earth, while Joe listened happily to all the details of the visit that had swept away the last shadow of misunderstanding between his sister and his dearest friend.

"You were right, Joe, when you said that five minutes' talk, face to face, would wipe out all misunderstanding," said Jim. "Why, in less than five minutes after I saw her I was the happiest fellow on earth. If you could have seen the way she flew to me!"

"What about that Pepperil?" asked Joe.

"Never was in it for a minute," declared Jim, happily. "Of course, the poor man was in love with her; but you can't blame him for that. Who wouldn't be? As a matter of fact, I think he was trying to propose to her at the time I got there. But she forgot he was alive when she saw me. You see, she'd simply tolerated him for the sake of your father's invention that Pepperil had arranged to finance. She couldn't be rude to him for fear of injuring the deal, though he bored her to death. What with the nuisance of his hanging around there and your father's anxiety about his invention and your mother's sickness and the cares of the household bearing down upon her, the poor girl was nearly crazy. Told me that when she sat down to write to me her head was in such a whirl that she hardly knew what she was writing. That's why her letters sometimes seemed so abstracted and unsatisfying. But now the deal has gone through, your mother's getting steadily better, Pepperil's sailing for Europe, and we're going to be married as soon as the baseball season is over."

"Fine!" cried Joe, his eyes beaming.

"And to think that I ever doubted her for a minute!" Jim berated himself. "Joe, I'm the meanest hound dog that ever lived. I'm not fit for such a girl. Why, Joe, she's——"

"Yes, I know," interrupted the grinning Joe. "Write me a letter and describe her perfections in that. But honestly, Jim, I'm as happy as you are."

"You can't be!" declared Jim. "It isn't possible for any one to be as happy as I am."

"Well, only a little less happy," corrected Joe. "And there's some one else that will be just as happy as I am. Mabel will be in the seventh heaven. She's worried herself sick."

"Too bad."

"Feel fit to pitch now?" asked Joe, after a while.

"Fit?" cried Jim. "That's no word for it. Bring on your teams. They'll all look alike to me."

And Jim proved in the games that followed that this was no idle boast. He was superb, the old invincible Jim, toying with his opponents and turning in victory after victory. McRae rubbed his eyes and Robbie chortled in glee.

"Sure, Mac, 'twas the best thing you ever did, letting Jim off to see that girl of his," said Robbie. "'Tis a new man he is since he came back."

The Giants were now like a team of runaway horses. They could not be stopped. With their pitching staff going at top speed, the team played behind them like men possessed. At home or on the road made no difference. The Giants were simply bent on having that pennant, and they strode over everything in their way.

They kept their stride without faltering, and in the last weeks of the season were rapidly closing in on the Chicagos, who were struggling desperately to maintain their lead.

On the last Western trip, their strongest opposition was encountered in Pittsburgh, and they had to exert themselves to the utmost.

The first game resulted in a Giant victory by a close margin, the visiting team just managing to nose through after a terrific struggle.

Just after the game had ended, Jackwell made a sudden rush for the grandstand. Bowen, to whom he had shouted, was close behind him.

Joe and Jim followed to see what it was all about, and found a stout, red-faced man in the grasp of the two athletes, while a policeman was edging his way through the crowd.

"Arrest this man!" cried Jackwell, to the officer. "He's a swindler. His name is Bromley, and he's wanted in Texas. Detectives have been searching all over the country for him."

The man denied it, but Jackwell persisted. The officer turned uncertainly to Joe.

"I don't know the man," said Joe. "But I know that the federal agents are after a man named Bromley. If this isn't the man, he can easily establish his identity at headquarters. These men seem to be pretty sure of him."

The officer put his hand on the man's arm.

"Better come with me and see the Chief," he said, and the man, still protesting, was led away. Later, federal agents identified him as the man wanted, and Jackwell and Bowen split the five thousand dollar reward between them.

"Glad those boys have settled their account with that rascal," remarked Joe, after the crowd had dispersed.

"Yes," replied Jim. "I wish we could say as much."

"You mean with the McCarney crowd?"

"Just that. My blood fairly boiled when I saw those scoundrels in the stand this afternoon."

"Were they there?" asked Joe.

"Very much there! Heads close together and talking all the time. Probably hatching up some other plan to down you. I tell you, Joe, you're in danger every minute that you're in this town!"

CHAPTER XXIX

THE SNAKE'S HEAD

"I suppose I am," replied Joe, impressed by the earnestness of Jim's tone. "It's up to us to keep our eyes open. Luckily, we have only three more days to stay here. All I want is to have them keep away from me till the season's ended. Then the tables will be turned, and I'll get after them."

Joe and Jim changed into their street clothes and came out of the clubhouse. All the other men had gone, except Iredell, who had not quite finished dressing.

"Dandy weather," remarked Joe, as they lingered for a moment on the steps. "What do you say, Jim, to a little auto ride to-morrow morning, along the Lincoln pike? Splendid road and fine scenery."

"I'm on," assented Jim. "I'd like nothing better."

The weather was perfect the next day, and shortly after breakfast the chums hired a speedy little car and set out for their ride. The machine purred along smoothly, with Joe at the wheel, and as travelers were comparatively few at that early hour, they had the road largely to themselves, and on the long stretches could let the car out to an exhilarating speed.

"This is the life!" exclaimed Jim, jubilantly, as he settled back in his seat and drew in long breaths of the invigorating air. "It does a fellow good sometimes to — Look out, Joe! Look out!"

His shout of alarm was torn from him by a great motor truck that came darting at high speed from a side road that had been partially concealed by trees and underbrush.

It came thundering down upon the little car as though it were bent on annihilating it.

Joe's quick glance took in the danger, and he swerved sharply to one side. Not sharply enough, however, to escape the impact altogether. The truck caught the car a glancing blow that hurled it like a catapult against a fence at the side of the road, which at that point ran along the edge of a deep ravine.

The car crashed through the fence, and had it not been that one of the wheels struck the trunk of a tree, would have plunged headlong into the gulch. The blow slewed the machine around, where it hung partly over the edge.

Jim had been thrown against the windshield and his hands were cut by the flying glass. Joe had clung desperately to the wheel, and though badly shaken up, had sustained no injury.

Without waiting to see the extent of the damage, the truck had gone on at breakneck speed. By the time the young men had leaped to the ground, the truck had vanished around a turn in the road.

Joe and Jim looked at each other, pale with anger.

"Are you hurt, Jim?" asked Joe, as he saw the blood on his comrade's hands.

"Only scratches," was the reply. "And I'm so thankful I'm not dead that I don't mind little things like that."

"It's almost a miracle that we're not lying at this moment at the bottom of the ravine," said Joe, soberly. "What do you think of those fellows? Did you ever see such reckless driving?"

"It wasn't reckless," declared Jim, grimly. "It was deliberate. That fellow was trying to run us down."

"What?" exclaimed Joe.

"Just that," reiterated Jim. "Did you see the man who was driving?"

"No," said Joe. "I only saw the truck. I was too busy trying to get the car out of the way to notice the driver."

"Well, I saw him," said Jim. "That is, I saw part of him. He had his coat drawn up and his cap pulled down so as to hide his face. But I caught sight of the biggest pair of lob ears I ever saw on any man. Does that mean anything to you?"

"Lemblow!" exclaimed Joe.

"Lemblow," assented Jim. "And probably the rest of the gang were in the truck back of him. I tell you, Joe, those fellows are out to do you. They failed in their first attempt, and so they tried this."

"And they came mighty near putting this across," said Joe. "But how on earth did they know we were going on this ride? We didn't mention it to anybody."

"No," agreed Jim, "not directly. But when we first spoke of it yesterday afternoon, we were on the clubhouse steps. Iredell was still in there, dressing, and the door was open."

"By George, you've hit it!" cried Joe. "Jim, the time has come for a showdown. We won't wait till the end of the season. We may not see the end of the season if this kind of thing is allowed to go on. I'm going to get even with those scoundrels before we leave Pittsburgh."

"I'm with you till the cows come home," declared Jim. "I'm aching to get my hands on them. But how are you going to do it?"

"By shadowing Iredell," replied Joe. "It's a dead certainty that he'll meet the rest of the gang to talk things over before we leave the city. We'll keep him in sight every night from now on and follow him to their meeting place. Then we'll trim the bunch."

"Good dope!" ejaculated Jim. "And now let's get this car out to the side of the road where the owners can send for it. There'll be a good-sized dent in our bankrolls by the time we get through paying for the damage."

They took care not to speak of the incident to any one, and at the game that afternoon showed no antipathy or suspicion in regard to Iredell. Several times they noticed the covert glances of that individual directed toward Jim's scratched hands—glances in which malignity was mingled with disappointment—but they gave no sign, and conducted themselves exactly as usual.

But not for a moment was Iredell out of their sight without their knowing where he was. All their faculties were intent upon using him as an unwitting guide to the rendezvous of the gang.

For a time after supper, Iredell hung around the lobby of the hotel. It was nearly ten o'clock before he sauntered carelessly into the street, where Joe and Jim were ensconced in the shadow of convenient doorways.

Iredell walked along slowly at first, glancing about from side to side, but as he saw nothing to arouse his suspicion, he quickened his steps and soon was making rapidly for the outskirts of the city. Joe and Jim followed at some distance, keeping in the shadows as much as possible.

In a little while they found themselves in a cheap quarter of the city, not far from the bank of the Allegheny River. Factories and slag heaps alternated with shabby dwellings, dimly lighted stores, and low resorts.

Standing in a lot, with no houses for a considerable distance on either side, was an old one-story shack. From its battered and dilapidated appearance, it seemed unfit for human habitation. But that some one was in it was indicated by the light from a smoky oil lamp that threw a flickering beam through the open window.

Iredell pushed his way along the weed-grown path and knocked three times. After a moment the door was opened and Iredell entered.

Joe and Jim waited for a brief time, and then, with the stealth of Indians, crept up near the open window. Bushes were growing all around the house, and behind these the two friends crouched. The brushwood was so thick that they were perfectly safe from detection, while at the same time they had a clear vision of the room and its inmates.

They had no difficulty in identifying the latter. Hupft, McCarney, Lemblow and Iredell were seated around a table, engaged in an excited conversation.

There was practically no other furniture in the room than the table and chairs. It was evident that none of the gang lived there, but that they had picked out an abandoned house where they could meet in security and talk with freedom.

There was no attempt to lower their voices, and the unseen listeners had no difficulty in hearing every word that was said.

"So we've made another flivver," growled McCarney, pounding the table angrily with his fist.

"Seems so," said Iredell, moodily. "They turned up at the game this afternoon just as though nothing had happened. Barclay had some scratches on his hand, but Matson was unhurt. At least he didn't show any signs of injury."

"I'm beginning to think we can't down that fellow," muttered Hupft. "No matter what we do, he comes up smiling."

"Nonsense!" snarled Lemblow. "He's had luck, that's all. The pitcher that goes to the well too often is broken at last. There's luck in odd numbers, and the third time we'll get him."

Joe felt in his pocket and took out an object that was roughly oblong in shape. He gripped it tightly in his hand and waited.

Jim, who had noted the action, reached out and touched his friend's arm.

"What's the game?" he whispered.

"You'll see in a minute," returned Joe. "When I start, you follow me."

"Lemblow's right," cried McCarney, rising to his feet, his face inflamed with passion. "We've failed twice, but the third time we'll get him. We'll get him so hard — —"

He never finished the sentence.

Something whizzed through the open window with terrific force and caught him right between the eyes. Taken by surprise, and partly stunned by the force of the blow, he went down heavily to the floor.

With startled shouts, the other three leaped to their feet and stood staring at the table on which the missile had fallen. Iredell leaned forward, took one look and jumped back with a terrified yell.

"It's a rattlesnake's head!" he screamed in horror.

His shriek was echoed by the other rascals as they fell back from the table, trembling as though with palsy.

The next instant, Joe and Jim, who had jumped through the window, were upon the rascals, dealing out blows with the force of trip-hammers. Iredell went down from a terrific right on the chin, and lay motionless. Hupft and Lemblow tried to fight back, but their nerves were so unstrung and they had been so overwhelmed with surprise at the sudden onslaught that their efforts were pitiful. Joe and Jim, all their pent up indignation putting double strength into their muscular arms, gave them the beating of their lives, until they cowered in a corner, covering their faces with their hands and whimpering for mercy.

"I guess that will do, Jim," said Joe at last. "They'll carry the marks of this for a long time, and they'll remember this night as long as they live.

"Now listen to me, you rascals," he said, with withering scorn, as his eyes bored through the discomfited conspirators. "What you've got to-night isn't a circumstance to what's coming to you if you ever dare to lift a finger against me again. I could have every one of you arrested and put behind bars for years to come if I wanted to, but I prefer to settle my own quarrels. But just one more move on your part, and you'll go where the dogs won't bite you for a while.

"As for you, Iredell," he continued, in a slightly gentler tone, addressing his teammate who was now sitting up on the floor, still half dazed, "I could have you fired off the team in disgrace and blacklisted forever, if I told McRae of this dirty work of yours. But I remember that you have a family and that you've played on the same team with me for years, and I'm going to give you one more chance. No one will hear of this if you go straight from now on. Cut out these dogs of companions and play the game like a man.

"Come along, Jim," he concluded, "I guess our night's work is done. We'll leave the snake's head behind as a souvenir."

The night's work was indeed done, and done so effectively that Joe suffered no more trouble from the precious trio. As for Iredell, the lesson had been sufficient, and while there never was a resumption of the cordial relations of previous years, he gave no further cause for complaint. At the end of the season he was traded, as young Renton had filled his place so well that the Giants could do without him.

The Giants "cleaned up" in Pittsburgh, and did so well with the other teams that the last day of the season found them tied with Chicago for the lead. The Cubs had played out all their games. The Giants still had one to play with Brooklyn. If they won, they would have the pennant. If they lost, the flag would go to Chicago.

CHAPTER XXX

THE FINAL BATTLE

The game was to be played on the Polo Grounds, and excitement was at fever heat. It seemed as though the whole male population of Greater New York had determined to see that game. Men waited in line all night, and from early morning the surface cars and elevated trains were packed with people going to the grounds.

The weather was fair, and the lovers of the game had a day that was all that could be desired. The turf had been rolled and groomed till it looked like green velvet.

The odds were in the Giants' favor, because they were the stronger team and because they were playing on their own grounds. Still, they had been whipped by the same team before on the same grounds, and they might be again. And the nervous tension they were under because of the importance of the game made them the more liable to break at critical points in the contest. The Brooklyns, on the other hand, had nothing to lose, and for that very reason might be the cooler-headed.

McRae had picked Joe as his pitching "ace" for this deciding contest. Grimm had been selected as the boxman for the delegation from across the bridge. At the moment, he was going better than any other of the Dodgers' staff, and any team that whipped him would know at least that it had been in a fight.

But on that day Joe feared no pitcher in the League. He was in magnificent shape in mind and body. In the preliminary practice with Mylert he made the latter wince, as the balls came over smoking hot.

"Save that stuff for the Brooklyns, Joe," Mylert protested, "or you'll have me a cripple before the bell rings."

Not only Joe's arm but his heart felt good that day. Mabel was sitting in a box, watching him proudly, and he felt that he simply couldn't lose. She was his mascot, and he carried near his heart the little glove that had rested there when he won the championship of the world.

Beside her sat Clara, flushed and happy and as sweet as a rose. She had come on from Riverside, bringing the glad news that Mrs. Matson was making astonishing progress and had now almost entirely regained her health.

So it was with a mind at peace and spirits high that Joe faced the doughty sluggers of the team from across the big bridge.

From the very start, it was apparent that he had "everything." Never had he been in finer form. Brain and muscle worked in perfect unison. Every ball he pitched had a reason behind it. He knew the weaknesses of every batter, and played upon them. The man who was death on low balls got a high one, and vice versa. His speed, his change of pace, his curve, his fadeaway, his hop, his control—all of these obeyed him as though under the spell of a magician. If ever a man made a ball "talk," Joe did that day.

Again and again the Brooklyns switched their tactics. Sometimes they lashed out at the first ball pitched. Again they tried to wait him out. These failing, they resorted to bunting. Nothing was of any avail. They were simply up against unhittable pitching.

Inning after inning went by without a score. In the fourth, Naylor made a scratch, and in the seventh, Leete hit the ball for a clean single. But on these occasions, Joe tightened up, and no man got as far as second, despite the desperate efforts of their comrades to advance the runner.

Grimm, too, was pitching fine ball, but not by any means airtight. The Giants had gotten to him for six hits, but, with one exception, no two had been allowed in the same inning, and the Giants were as scoreless as their opponents.

Grimm had thought discretion the better part of valor when Joe had faced him, and had twice passed him deliberately to first. The boos of the spectators failed to disturb Grimm's equanimity. His motto was "safety first." On a third occasion, his cunning miscarried, and Joe, walking into the ball in desperation, had clouted it for a two baser. But as two were out at the time and the next man fanned, he was left holding second.

In the ninth, Joe put on extra steam and fanned three men in a row, amid the cheers of the Giant rooters.

Then the Giants came in for their last half. Grimm made Burkett hit a grounder to first that was an easy out. Larry sent a Texas leaguer behind second that was gathered in by the guardian of that bag. Then Joe came to the bat.

Grimm still had no mind to give him a hit, and the first two balls were wide of the plate. He tried to put the third in the same place, but his control faltered and the ball came within Joe's reach.

There was a mighty crash, and the ball started on a line between right and center. At the crack of the bat, Joe was off like a frightened jackrabbit. He rounded first and started for second.

Out of the corner of his eye, he saw the right- and centerfielders running for the ball, which had struck the ground and was rolling toward the wall. He knew that it would rebound, and that one of the fielders would "play the angle," and thus get it the sooner.

The people in the stands had risen now, and were shouting like madmen. He caught just one glimpse of Mabel, standing in her box with her hands pressed on her heart.

He made second and kept on for third. On and on he went, as though on wings. His heart beat like a trip hammer. His lungs seemed as though they would burst. The wind whistled in his ears. He had never run like that in his life.

He rounded third and made for home. The ball was coming, as he knew from the shouts of the spectators and the warning yells of his comrades. Down that white stretch he tore. He saw the catcher set himself for the coming ball, knew from his eyes that the ball was near. With one mighty leap, he threw himself to the ground in a marvelous hook slide that swung his body out of the catcher's reach and yet just permitted his outstretched fingers to touch the plate before the catcher put the ball on him.

"Safe!" cried the umpire. The game was won, the pennant cinched, and the Giants once more were the champions of the National League.

What Mabel thought of Joe she told him privately. What McRae and Robbie and his teammates thought of him they told him publicly. What the newspapers thought of him they told the world. As pitcher, as batter, and as captain, Baseball Joe was proclaimed the king of them all.

And what Mr. and Mrs. Matson, the former happy because of the success of his invention, the latter because of her restoration to health, thought of their famous son they told to him a few weeks later at a wedding ceremony in the Riverside home, when Clara placed her hand in Jim's and made him the happiest of men.

THE END

9 781836 572787